Phoebe M Feilden

Grantham Secrets

A novel. Part 1

Phoebe M Feilden

Grantham Secrets
A novel. Part 1

ISBN/EAN: 9783337065553

Printed in Europe, USA, Canada, Australia, Japan

Cover: Foto ©Andreas Hilbeck / pixelio.de

More available books at **www.hansebooks.com**

GRANTHAM SECRETS.

A Novel.

BY

PHŒBE M. FEILDEN.

IN THREE VOLUMES.

VOL. I.

London:

SAMUEL TINSLEY,

10, SOUTHAMPTON STREET, STRAND.

1875.

GRANTHAM SECRETS.

CHAPTER I.

"What a glorious moon! Oh, mother, what a night! I wish we might walk on for ever, instead of having to stop short at Grantham Hall!"

So cried Margaret Willoughby, as she opened the side-door of a pleasant house which went by the name of "The Cottage," and followed her mother out into the delicious August air.

For a moment the two stood gazing, as though spell-bound by the beauty of the scene which they had so frequently gazed at before. Then turning a little to their left, they bent their steps across a soft sloping lawn towards a piece of rougher

ground which took to a path winding
through a small wood, the ups and downs
of which led the way to a little wicket gate
opening upon the private property of Sir
John Grantham, the lord of the manor.

"How wonderful it looks!" said Margaret, stopping, soon after they had reached
the wood, to feast her eyes and her fancy
on shadowy corners, which appeared to be
endless in their mysterious depths, and on
rich moonbeams which, as they fell amidst
the shade, lit up here and there a fern, a
flower, or a moss-grown stone, and seemed
to be revealing a thousand treasures which
had been kept secret during the sunshine
of day. In short, the pretty spot had been
transformed for Margaret into a land of
marvellous enchantment. And, may be,
her fancies might have remained entranced
by it till cock-crow, but for the necessity of
obeying her mother's impatient call.

"My child, we shall be very late. Do
you mean to stay dreaming here all night?"

"It seems a sin to leave the wood for a
tiresome house," replied Margaret, half to

herself, "It never looked so lovely, or gave me such a strange feeling before. I feel as if something wonderful must be going to happen."

"I know what is about to happen," returned her mother. "We are going to receive a scolding from Lady Grantham for being fashionable, and to find that the dancing has begun, and that you have lost all chance of partners!"

"I am not much afraid, mother. Mr. Meredith will of course be there, and may perhaps have kept a dance or two for me," said Margaret, with a careless laugh; adding, with a shrug of her shoulders, and a grimace expressive of mingled amusement and disgust, "and that Miles Grantham, too! I suppose he will allow me the great honour and delight of dancing with him occasionally. But I must make Mr. Meredith save me from this, if I can."

"My dear!" began Mrs. Willoughby.

"Well, mamma, you must agree with me in thinking Miles Grantham hateful! He always seems to me like a wicked sprite in a

German fairy-tale," put in Margaret, hastily.
And then, while her mother continued her
expostulations, her quick fancy peopled an
imaginary world with ideal beings, who,
although not fairies, were certainly utterly
unlike any actual creatures of flesh and
blood with whose characters she had as
yet become acquainted. This fanciful world,
in which it was the wont of her imagination
to take frequent refuge, just now harmonized
well with the charm and beauty of the soft
moonlit evening; and her ideal friends
seemed unusually living, and unusually
full of interest, as she compared them with
the "commonplace" people whom she was
about to meet at Grantham Hall. Above
all, the chief hero of her imagination,—he
who took the most prominent place in the
pictures painted by her brain, he who was
the principal mover in the scenes of action
that her fancy had created,—appeared to-
night to have been inspired with new vir-
tues, and to have been endowed with more
extraordinary powers! It was impossible
that she could ever meet his like on earth,

she thought!—one who was at once so self-sacrificing, so manly, so true, so skilful, and at the same time so fascinating, so nobly beautiful, so humorous, so capable of entering into all moods, whether grave or gay! But, although this was impossible, apparently it was none the less fair and just that Margaret's acquaintances should bear the penalty of her contempt and displeasure because they were so far from approaching the likeness of her own lofty ideal.

With this ideal moving before her mind's eye, amidst the many glowing fancies that made her inner life delightful, Margaret accompanied her mother into the large drawing-room of Grantham Hall. The other guests had already assembled. The party was not large. It was one of those informal meetings for dancing and music, round games and friendly conversation, for which the hospitable inhabitants of Grantham Hall were famous. These parties were usually got up suddenly. The neighbours were asked in an *impromptu* manner to spend the evening at the Hall. No one

felt obliged to accept the invitation merely
because he had no previous engagement.
But few who had ever attended a "Grantham evening," as it was termed in the
neighbourhood, were disposed to disregard
the chance of attending another. And sad-
hearted, indeed, must that young person
have been who failed to enjoy it when it
came. For certainly the host and hostess
had the art of infusing their own genial
spirit into the minds of their guests. All
were made to feel at their ease; and everything went brightly and pleasantly during
the two or three hours that the entertainment lasted. Nor was any one happier on
an occasion of the sort than Margaret
Willoughby, who, despite the superiority
of her own waking dream-land, found outer
life at Grantham Hall exceedingly agreeable. Of course the commonplace and
uninteresting people whom she met there
could not be of any great consequence to
one who was accustomed to hold intercourse
with a far nobler race of beings, of her own
creation; but nevertheless it could not be

otherwise than satisfactory to find herself
welcomed so heartily, and looked upon as
so necessary an element in other people's
enjoyment. She was fuller of fun and
merriment than any of the other girls; and
her arrival at the present moment was
hailed with delight by all.

"Here they are at last!" exclaimed Lady
Grantham, as she shook hands with Mrs.
Willoughby, and then turned an involuntarily
admiring glance on her daughter's radiant
face.

Margaret was generally considered rather
to be winning, graceful, and picturesque than
actually pretty, but there was something
about her as she entered now that made
those who looked at her say to themselves,
"How beautiful! She is absolutely beautiful!"

In truth, her countenance had been transfigured into unwonted beauty by the brightness of the thoughts and fancies that were
working within her mind. She was little
aware, however, of the effect she was pro
ducing while she passed quickly through

the room, and, joining a group of acquaintances, charmed them all by her simple and
natural manner, and her ready sympathy
with them in all they had to tell of their
doings and concerns.

"You will give me a dance?" suddenly
whispered some one close behind her, in a
tone as low, mysterious, and tender as
though the request he was making had been
one of a somewhat more important nature.

A shade of annoyance crossed Margaret's
face, but turning quickly round,—

"How do you do, Miles?" she said, in a
cheerful, abrupt, and unconcerned manner.
"I did not see you. I beg your pardon!
Were you saying something to me?"

"You did not see me! You did not
know that I was near!" with a softly reproachful intonation in his accents, returned
Miles Grantham.

"Of course I did not know that you were
near when I did *not* see you. How should
I?" said Margaret, in a voice that was less
gentle and sweet than usual.

Miles' answer was a sigh, but he added,

with lips that seemed to be tremulous from emotion,—

"You will not surely refuse me a dance?"

"Why should I refuse you a dance?" replied Margaret, with an impatient laugh. "Of course it would be the death of you if I did! But, luckily for you, bare civility forbids me to be your murderer. I have no engagement, and shall be happy to dance with you as soon as you have fulfilled all yours."

"Mine! Ah, you remind me of my duty! You remind me of that stern taskmaster, my duty!" And once more heaving a sigh, Miles glanced in the direction of a group of young ladies who were waiting impatiently for the music of the next waltz to strike up.

Margaret's eyes danced with merriment, while a pensive-looking young lady, who had caught Mr. Grantham's glance, blushed, lowered her eyelids, and thought to herself, "Yes, I am sure I cannot be mistaken! That look—those tones—must surely mean something! But of course he cannot help himself: of course he must pay attentions to others besides me! He is not one to let his own feelings interfere with his duty!"

Some one sat down to the piano and began to play a waltz, but still Miles Grantham lingered by Margaret's side.

"Your partner is waiting for you. You must 'go where duty calls you,' you know!" returned Margaret, mischievously.

"And you?" he said, in a tone of despondency, as he prepared at length to leave her.

"And *I* may possibly contrive to exist for a short time without you!" answered Margaret. Then murmuring to herself an ejaculation of thanksgiving at his departure, she retreated into a corner of the bay, and sat down by the open window. "I wonder if he fancies that I don't know that he speaks in the same sweet tone (as *they* may consider it!) to every other girl in the place!" she mused, while with contemptuous amusement she watched Miles Grantham's tall, stooping, narrow-chested figure make its way to the side of his expectant partner, and observed how she raised confiding eyes to his dark sallow face, and returned his insinuating smile with one of grateful contentment. "Is it possible that the being lives on earth who finds herself able to worship *that* thing? Better be one of the ' poor ignorant heathen' at once, for their idols have at least the virtue of being dumb !'"

After this fashion Margaret continued her musings, expressing to herself the senti- ments and opinions in which she was almost singular. For with the ladies of the neigh- bourhood, generally, Miles Grantham had contrived to make himself popular. The mothers thought him an agreeable and ex- emplary young man. To the young ladies he was a hero of romance, possessed of every virtue under the sun. In their eyes the long features (which really were not ill- formed) appeared extraordinarily handsome. In the contracted brow they could see nothing amiss. And the fact that he was possessed by an apparent inability to look anyone steadily in the face only made him seem the more interesting ; for to each one the self-conscious droop of his eyelids seemed full of a thousand tender meanings, which only the fear of giving offence to her prevented his expressing in direct looks and words. One of these furtive, hurried glances of his, spoke volumes to the fertile imaginations of his young lady friends. And even the men of his acquaintance usually declared to themselves, after a time, that the heir of Grantham had "something in him," after all, and was "less of a muff" than they had fancied.

Can it have been that a too great familiarity had bred contempt in Margaret's mind? This is so far possible that Margaret and Miles had been playfellows in their childhood. All her life long, ever since the days when the big effeminate boy had lorded it over the little child whom he had been ordered to amuse, Margaret had been bored by Miles' show of affection, annoyed by his exigence and tyranny, and disgusted by his petty, mean, and cunning ways, his intense self-importance and offensive egoism. In their youthful quarrels her mother had

always told her that she, not the boy, who
was so much older than herself, was the one
to blame. And the only person from whom
she had obtained, in those days, relief from
her sense of injustice was Sir John Grantham,
whose dislike towards his nephew and heir,
though struggled against and kept locked
up a secret in his own bosom, was almost
equal to her own.

On one point, however, at all events,
Margaret wronged her old playfellow. It
is true that it was his glorious aim to make
each young lady in the neighbourhood of
Grantham believe that he was in love with
her, and with her alone. But it is no less
certain that it was his earnest intention to
make Margaret Willoughby the future mistress of Grantham Hall. Nor, in his vain
self-confidence, did he dream of resistance,
on her part, to his sovereign will and
pleasure.

"Poor Alice Craycroft! He shall marry
her, as certainly as he was made to keep the
daffodil he had chosen, when he cunningly
tried to exchange it for my lily of the valley,

in the days of our childish fights. Dear old
Nurse Gilling came to the rescue then.
How well I remember her look! I can see
her now, and hear her, giving it to Miles,
and saying it was a shame of a great big
boy like that, " what called himself a young
gentleman," trying to cheat a little young
lady like Miss Margaret out of her flower!
Yes, he shall marry Alice to a certainty.
Only, poor dear Alice, will she continue to
be blinded, and to dream that her ape is a
god ? "

Thus Margaret continued her musings,
while she clenched her little white hands
together, and looked with a determined air
in the direction of Miles and his pensive
partner, who were spinning round to the
music of the Elfin Waltzes.

But her musings and her determined
thoughts were speedily interrupted. The
sound of footsteps approaching the window
from without made her turn her head to
see the youthful and yet manly figure of
Charles Meredith, who, hastening up to her,
greeted her in a voice of frank gladness.

There was nothing remarkable or hero-like in his appearance; he was simply exceedingly nice-looking, with a broad well-formed brow, truth-telling dark eyes, and a pleasant straightforward expression of countenance.

"How long have you been here, Miss Willoughby?" he said. "I have been looking for you. How did I manage to miss you?"

"We came through the wood, and then took the short cut to the avenue; mamma was afraid we were late."

"You are,—very late. Shall we have this waltz?"

"With pleasure."

"Have you many engagements? I have none. Can you spare me some more dances?"

"I am engaged for a waltz with Mr. Grantham."

"But not the next? Oh, it seems this is to be a quadrille on the lawn. Shall we dance it?"

So they danced and promenaded on the lawn, and even waltzed again, without being disturbed by Miles Grantham. The music was good. They both danced well, and seemed to have been made to fit into each other's movements. They talked and laughed together between whiles. And Margaret was completely and carelessly gay and happy.

CHAPTER II.

AND CHARLES? Was his happiness equally light and equally devoid of care? Were there no hidden depths of love in his heart, mingling with the throbbings of a mighty fear, which made it both joy and agony inexpressible to him to be by her side—which made her sweet unconscious merriment at once a pain and a pleasure which something told him he must shortly lose? For she was unconscious, unconscious of anything beyond the pleasant sense of being liked in a friendly, hearty, and genial manner.

Four or five weeks had passed since Charles had settled himself down in the neighbourhood for the ostensible purpose of reading hard for his Oxford degree. Mr. Meredith was particularly anxious that

his son should try for honours. And
Charles, who possessed little or no personal ambition, and who hated close study,
—except in connection with any subject in
which his eager mind happened for the
time being to be feeling peculiar interest,
—was nevertheless determined to gratify
his father; and, with this object in view,
he had taken up his position in a retired
country spot, in a small cottage close to
a good trout stream. With the supersti-
tion of his kind, he had looked to much
assistance in his studies from the companionship of the neighbouring fish. But
he had expected no other diversion and
no other companionship than that which
they afforded him. Alas, for his good
intentions! He had fallen in with an
Oxford acquaintance, had been introduced
to Sir John Grantham, and had become a
victim to the hospitality and dissipation of
a very pleasant neighbourhood. And the
trout-stream, his books, his thoughts, his
dreams, all now were haunted by a girl's
small piquant face, and especially by its

great changeful hazel eyes, which to him
seemed the sweetest eyes that had ever
opened upon sky and earth. The waters
of his life which had hitherto flowed on in
a calm and even course had at length been
troubled to their depths, and in the troubling
had gained for him a higher and a dearer
value. Of all this, however, Margaret had
as yet learnt nothing. How was she to
gather anything of it from the frank and
buoyant, or simply grave, almost matter-of-
fact manner in which he discussed with her
all kinds of subjects connected with earth
and heaven? He had spoken to her no
word of love, and was not one of those who
by dint of tones and looks, or a nameless
something, have the power of impressing
themselves on the minds or hearts of others.
So, while he was fast becoming devoted to
her, she only experienced in his society an
agreeable divertisement, which it would not
materially affect her happiness to lose.
Even now, when following the lead of others
amongst the guests, they passed out into
the warm,—almost golden,—light of the har-

vest moon, and wandered, amongst other wanderers, through the pleasure-grounds, far down out of sight of the house, passing from glade to glade, talking of poetry, poets, and pictures, and pausing for an instant, from time to time, to admire and feel together the quiet loveliness around them,—even now no touch of romance or poetry coloured the placidity of her feeling for him. Even now, while she talked brightly, and gave full attention to her companion's observations and questions, it seemed to her that her spirit was living in an inner world, which she did not care to share with him. And thoughts were passing quickly through her mind, which none, she fancied, could understand, but the ideal hero, who existed only in her own imagination. This hero's thoughts, and not her own, they seemed to be; for Margaret had no egoism; she cared little to dwell on herself, and had no grand notions as to her personal mental powers or her own peculiar sentiments.

"I little thought how pleasant I should find it down here," abruptly said Charles

Meredith, presently. "It seemed hard lines to me, at first, having to stay in England for reading, instead of joining my people in Switzerland; but——"

"But," put in Margaret, laughingly, as he paused, "you now begin to feel the benefit of extraordinarily severe study."

"Well, I *have* been reading very hard, you know," said Charles, quickly, in a tone of half-serious, half-playful deprecation, and with a movement of his face that was something between a smile and a grimace. It was a look that Margaret knew well and liked to provoke. It amused her, because it was so quaint and peculiar, so characteristic of Charles, and of no one else. It pleased her, and yet it would have been utterly impossible for her ideal hero, her imaginary piece of perfection, to have given a similar look, or to have made a similar movement.

"Ah! I am afraid you will be worn to a skeleton soon. You really should take more care of yourself!" she returned.

"I am anxious to martyr myself for the

good of my friends," said Charles. "They may make something out of me, by-and-by, perhaps, by showing me as 'The Living Skeleton!' But, seriously, you know it is only to please my father that I care to go up for honours. What good will they do me, supposing me to be successful?"

How different from the hero! Margaret made her mental comparison to this effect, but only said aloud, "Will it not help you afterwards in your profession? You mean to be a barrister, you say?"

"As well that as anything else, perhaps," replied Charles, dejectedly. "But I have not yet made up my mind. My father wishes me to do something, although he can make me a sufficient allowance to enable me to live without. I only mean to hang by my eyelashes to my profession, however. But don't be shocked, Miss Willoughby! I do not mean to be idle; I hope——"

He paused. Hitherto, he had pictured to himself, in bright and glowing colours, a future literary life in London. But suddenly the life had faded out of the picture, and he

saw only a dark and desolate scene, unless,
—unless certain wild hopes of his should
chance to be fulfilled.

Margaret was looking up at him with an
expression in her face that seemed to mean,
—oh! what might it not mean? It expressed
earnest interest. It was at once bright, and
grave, and wondering; and at least, for
Charles Meredith, it was dangerously beautiful. Poor Charles! If he could have read
her mind, if he could have known that as
she gazed up into his face the eyes of her
imagination were seeing the ideal hero,
whose whole life was earnest, whose voca-
tion, whatever it might be, was to himself
sacred, would he then have dared to breathe
aloud the presumptuous hopes which now
came like waves surging thick and fast
through his brain and heart, and which it
seemed no longer possible to restrain within
the bounds of prudence?

"Miss Willoughby," he cried, suddenly,
in an altered tone, "may I speak to you?
I—I have something that I must say to you;"
he stammered, hardly knowing what he

uttered, almost feeling as if he were speaking out of a dream.

In a moment scales fell from Margaret's eyes. She knew all; she saw and understood, at last! She stood still for an instant, frightened. In that instant, turning her head, she saw that some of the rest of the wandering party were beginning to stroll back towards the house. She would have followed them. "Let us go back with the others. We ought to go back," is what she would have said. But instead of this, "Oh, please don't!" she cried, abruptly, in an imploring tone. "It has been so pleasant. Oh, please, please, don't spoil it!"

"I must speak,—you must hear me," he answered, vehemently; and she found herself impelled forward against her will, and obliged to listen to his passionately tender and earnest pleadings. It was as if a dream of love in his heart had suddenly been awakened to life and activity; and words, no longer faltering and diffident, but full of force and determination, came rushing like a torrent through his lips.

Margaret, meanwhile, walked tremblingly by his side, affected she knew not how, sensible of intense distress, that yet, in spite of herself, was mingled with a strange, new, most exquisite thrill of pleasure; which, however, quickly passed into a painful yearning after a vague indescribable something, that seemed to be floating somewhere within her vision, but far away out of her reach. It was one of those moments of excitement in which imagination, thought, and feeling work with unusual rapidity, and the image in Margaret's ideal world had suddenly awakened into a struggle after actual life, which might not, it appeared, be satisfied. But through all the minglings of her pain and pleasure, she felt positively convinced that she did not return Charles Meredith's feeling. She liked him. It was pleasant to her to be by his side. But love? —love such as his, love such as her imagination told her it would be possible for her, too, to feel, *if* it were possible for the right person for it to be created, — the very strength of his vehemence made her all the

more certain that such an experience was
very far from being hers at present. Voices,
showing some of the rest of the party to be
in close proximity, had again been heard, and
Charles had instinctively drawn Margaret
aside, into one of the many paths of the
wood that they had been skirting,—a branch
of the very same wood through which she
had so lately passed.—Presently they came
to a little trellis-work summer-house, where
they stopped short, he, at the same time,
pausing in his speaking, to look at her with
inquiring, pleading eyes.

Then she realized the pain that she must
give, and with a look that was inexpressibly
sad and pitiful, she answered, tremulously,
" I never dreamed of this.   I knew you liked
me, I felt that you were kind to me; but I
did not—I did not dream that you had
thought of me in this way.   Indeed, I am
not worthy of it, and I,—I cannot,—oh,
forgive me for causing you this pain ! "

Her voice was very gentle, tears filled her
eyes.   And as his hopes sank she seemed to
Charles ten thousand times dearer even than

she had seemed when first he had begun to
speak. He had listened breathlessly, trust-
ing for some word that might at least bring
to him a little glimmering of hope. But
now he replied, in a tone that was almost
stern in its calm hopelessness,—

"You cannot love me, I see. I was a fool
to think it possible you might."

"Indeed, you are too, too good," she
began; and as she hesitated, all the agony
of his disappointment came over him, and
he said, imploringly,—

"Can you give me *no* hope? Is it impossible that you might some time learn to
love me?"

She shook her head. "Not in the way
you mean," she said. "Not as you deserve.
But—but—I—I——"

What could she say to soothe and console
him? She felt—she knew—what he was
suffering. She felt that conventional words
about sisterly affection, friendship, thoughts
and prayers, would only mock him in his
grief. Her heart was full, but her imagination was telling her that the man ordained

to possess its love was not this man with whom she was now feeling so keenly.

"But why—why is it quite impossible that you may some time learn to love me?" he broke in, with almost fierce persistency. "Is there——?"

"I have never seen anyone that I could care about in that way," said Margaret, quickly, answering the jealous thought of his heart. "I think I never shall, for if I should, it would be some one who——"

Once more she paused. The look that he had seen before came into her eyes. The warm moonlight slanted across her somewhat upturned face. There was a short silence, and then, "I will tell you something," she said, suddenly, in a confiding tone, which filled his quickly-throbbing heart anew with jealous fears; "I will tell you something that I have told to no one else. All my life long I have had fancy people about me. They were children when I was a child, and now they are grown up. They are good, but never tiresome in their goodness,—good, and true, and delightful and pleasant. One of them, the best of all, was very brave, and kind, and gentle, as a boy. I loved him dearly then, he was so different from all the tiresome real boys that I knew; and now that he is grown up he is,—oh, I cannot say it to you! It seems to me as if I knew him really, and he helps me by being so good and great, and so earnest in his work. He does not do sometimes one thing, and sometimes another thing, just as the fancy takes him, as I do; but he has a work that he puts his whole heart into. He does not mind how much trouble it gives him. He does not feel the trouble. It is not for himself. It——"

Again she hesitated, afraid of giving utterance to the grave thought that was in her mind; then she continued eagerly,—

" It helps a world of people to be better and happier. And——"

Here she glanced suddenly up into his face, and something that she read there made her pause abruptly. Something new had come over him! He no longer appeared to her merely a pleasant, amiable,

negative sort of being. There was an
inspired look on his countenance, as though
he had just received a revelation, as though
he had heard a Voice from the Unseen, calling upon him to fulfil the office of a Prophet.
Margaret's heart beat fast, her cheeks
flushed, and it seemed to her, all in an instant, that she had been brought into the
presence of her ideal hero,—that the
shadowy creation of her fancy had become
an actual creature of flesh and blood. She
stood in momentary confusion, and Charles
was the first to break silence. In a low and
quiet tone, as though he had put aside his
wild hopes of happiness, and were only
waiting to learn what he must do, how he
might obey the new impulse that had been
given to him,—

"And what is the work," he asked, "what
is the work, Miss Willoughby, into which
your fancy friend puts his whole heart?"

How was Margaret to reply? Her en-
thusiasm for the ideal hero seemed to have
vanished, and she would have given worlds
to hear the new-found substantial reality

address her again in the same tone in which he had so lately spoken. But as he stood gazing at her, as though she was a goddess from whom he was to receive his commands, she answered, with quick excitement,—

" His work? " I scarcely know, in detail, what it is. But he forgets himself in it, like Shakespeare, and Turner, and Mendelssohn, —and as all great workers must forget themselves (*you* think they must? We were talking about it the other day, you remember?) ; and his whole life is like a beautiful poem."

" If only the thought of you might help my life to become like a beautiful poem, which you would care to read, I might better learn to bear the loss of my one hope of happiness," returned Charles, as she concluded.

" Not the thought of *me*," she faltered, for he seemed to her so godlike at the moment, that she was humiliated by the knowledge that he was looking up to her unworthy self with reverence.

" Forgive me, Miss Willoughby," he said, sadly, misinterpreting her meaning, " forgive me! I understand you fully. I shall not dream any longer that you are holding out to me a hope for the future, and I will try to look to that other help of which you tell me. But, whatever may happen to me, whatever changes may come, I shall never leave off loving you. I could not live if I had not you to love."

He turned away his head as though to hide from her sight the look of agony that had overspread his features.

" I," she began, after a pause, during which the intensity of her feelings had not allowed her to speak, " I——"

Who knows what blessed hope her hesitating answer might have bought to Charles? Who knows what he might have replied, and what she once more might have returned to him? Who knows but that angel hands might have drawn together their two hearts, and have opened the eyes of each to know all the secrets of the other, if—if a third person had not suddenly entered upon the scene, and brought the *tête-a-tête* to a premature conclusion?

"Oh, here you are, Margaret, at last!" cried some one in a querulous tone of voice, which was intended to be pathetic." I have been hunting for you high and low! Mrs. Willoughby says it is time to go, and I have obtained leave for one more dance, as you were out of the way when it came to your turn."

"My turn? Its time had not been specified, except in your own mind!" said Margaret, with a forced laugh. "Out of the way? But surely you and your partner were of our party when we wandered off, after the waltz on the lawn?"

"Yes, but I was back in time for the last waltz, and had thought you were following."

"We remained out longer, with some of the rest of the party."

"I promised Mrs. Willoughby to bring you back, now, at all events."

"All right, I suppose we had better come, then, "said Margaret, trying to speak in an unconcerned tone.

"Unless you are more pleasantly engaged,—too bad of you, Meredith, to

carry off my partner," went on Miles, looking with an aggrieved air from one to the
other, and offering his arm to Margaret,
with the manner of one who considered that
she was his personal property, and that it
would be a piece of unheard of impertinence
in any one who dared to dispute his right to
do what he chose with her.

In sheer nervousness, in the fear lest the
odious Miles should begin to imagine that
there was "something between" herself
and Charles Meredith, Margaret began a
laughing apology, and permitted herself to
be carried off with an apparently good
grace. But when Charles glanced at her,
he perceived on her face the tender glow
which he might have observed there before
the arrival of the intruder; and out of her
eyes still looked the tender wistfulness which
had been there also, though he had not seen
it, even when she was beginning the tremulous answer which Miles had interrupted.
And while she laughed and chatted, mechanically, with the man she so cordially
disliked, her heart was full,—oh that

Charles might have seen into its depths!—
her heart was full, and was aching with a
longing to be able to recall a lost opportunity. Charles, meanwhile, twisting and
turning her words in his memory, and thinking humbly of himself, teased and vexed his
mind with insupportable surmises. Was it
possible, he thought, that only a word from
Miles Grantham was needed, in order to
discover to Margaret Willoughby the reality
of her ideal hero! He believed Miles to be
a far better and cleverer fellow than himself. He believed him to be no muff, in
spite of his priggish manner, and effemimate
voice and appearance.

"And yet, how I hate the fellow!" he
thought. "Jealous, I suppose! Can it be
only this that makes him seem to me so
utterly offensive and distasteful? Am I a
mean brute? If he loves her and she loves
him, what am I, to——? But ugh!" Here,
with a sudden impatient contraction of his
face, and a tight clenching together of his
teeth, he paused abruptly in his magnani-
mous thoughts, and asked himself impetu-

ously, "Is it possible that she can love him, —that she can love *him?*"

Then again there was a reaction in his mind, while the inspiration, the noble impulse, which her words and looks had seemed to bring, came sweeping once more over his spirit.

"I will sound him," he thought, "and if I wrong him, if he is in earnest, if he is worthy of her, if he has made her love him, —for her sake I will forbear to interfere, for her sake I will be strong, for her sake I will try to rise into a better and higher life! And yet, and yet, what good is there in strength and nobleness, what good in any thing, if I may not have her, if I may not have her love?"

This,—amidst all his thoughts, while he kept in the rear, amidst his attempts at lively replies when appealed to by either of the two whom he imagined to be taken up with each other,—this expressed the strong undercurrent of feeling by which his aching heart was unceasingly oppressed.

Gaily laughing and talking, the three

entered the drawing-room. Music struck
up. And Margaret found herself being
whirled round in a waltz, which seemed at
once the most blissful and the most miserable that she had ever danced. A brighter
gleam of joy than any that had crossed the
horizon of her dreams had now darted,
meteor-like, across the path of her actual
life,—joy, surely, moreover, that would increase, joy of which she was to have her
fill! Such was the sweet tale which the
bewitching music seemed to be telling her,
with variations and repetitions which were
never otherwise than sweet! But there was
an undertone of sadness. For her memory
was haunted by words sadly spoken, and by
a look of sorrowful hopelessness. Oh, when
would the music cease? When should she
be freed from its tyranny, and have it in her
power to change those mournful looks, those
sad tones, into expressions of great hope
and overwhelming joy? Surely there never
was a waltz so interminable! When, when
would it come to an end? She felt instinctively, as she was wafted round, that her

movements were followed by a pair of sadly thoughtful eyes looking out from the bay window! She felt that that corner in the window contained for her all sorrow and all gladness,—she felt that all her world was there! Why had it not power at once to attract her to itself,—to break the nightmare thraldom by which she seemed to be bound? Presently a buzz of voices came round about her world, and then it migrated and seemed to pass away out of her sight; only she heard Sir John Grantham's full hearty voice, and knew that he was talking to Charles; and but for the music, she might have caught fragments of their conversation as it ran thus,—

"Plenty more to show you in these parts. You must not run away from us yet awhile. You were never here before, I think you said?"

"Except that I had the honour of being born somewhere about here, two-and-twenty years ago."

"Oh, ay! Ay, ay! Two-and-twenty years ago!" A pause here, while Sir

John put his hand across his eyes, and
looked for a moment into the past. "Two-
and-twenty years ago!" he mused. "My
boy might have been just such another, just
such another as this one!" And then he
knitted his brows and angrily strained his
eyes in the direction of the, in his opinion,
unworthy heir apparent to Grantham Hall
and the Grantham baronetcy. "Nothing
of my poor brother about him! That cunning, cringing face is Madam all over!"

Thus for the thousandth time ran Sir
John's vexed and regretful thoughts on the
subject of his much-despised nephew. But
in another instant his voice was again to be
heard in pleasant laughter and genial talk.

The music ceased at last. The waltz
was over. Magaret's heart leaped into her
mouth. The moment of longed-for liberty
had surely arrived at length.

"My dear child, it is late, we must be
off." Mrs. Willoughby, as she spoke, rose
from the chair on which she had been seated
near Lady Grantham, with whom she had
been confabbing earnestly on a subject that

the two ladies were never weary of discussing, and hastened across the room to Margaret's side.

"I have not many fears," she had been
saying to Lady Grantham,—"I have not
many fears," she had said, while the sounds
of the final chord of the *finale* waltz were
dying away; "the child is frank and pleasant in her manner to other young men,
but evidently her heart is given to your
dear Miles."

"And she could not give it to one more
worthy of her regard, though I say it that
should not!" had Lady Grantham returned.
"I am sure his attention to me,—the way
he tries to supply the place of a son to his
childless aunt,"—a shake of the head and
a sigh had finished the sentence, and then,—

"You are tired, dear Lady Grantham.
We must be going!" had prefaced Mrs.
Willoughby's words of summons to her
daughter. "It is late, we must be off."

"Yes, mother, yes, in a moment," answered Margaret, dreamily, while she with-
drew her hand from Miles Grantham's arm,

and looked with a longing despair towards the opposite end of the room.

A crowd of young ladies, their partners and their mammas, divided her from Charles Meredith. Their voices sounded shrilly discordant in her ears; but over and above all the buzz and small-talk, she could hear Lady Grantham commend to Charles's care myriads of ladies who needed cloaking, refreshment, and an escort home. She could hear Charles' forced laugh and unavoidable words of courtesy, and could see the side-looks of dismay with which he prepared to fulfil the duties allotted to him.

" You have had nothing to eat. You will let me—" began Miles, in his most tiresome tones.

" Nothing, thanks," sharply interrupted Margaret.

" Then, my dear, come and get your cloak on at once," put in her mother, decidedly; and poor Margaret found herself being led with her mother, first into the cloak-room, and then out through the hall-door, down the beech-avenue, across a bit of lawn,

and through the wood; Miles Grantham
being their faithful escort all the way to The
Cottage. No matter! He might have been
leagues away for all the difference he made
to Margaret, who was wholly engrossed by
her own thoughts. With restless longing,
she recapitulated her conversation with
Charles, shaping her answers far differently
from what they had been, and, in imagination, making an ending, ah, how sweet, how
full of satisfaction! Then, with a sudden
rush of delicious hope, she looked forward
to the next day, when all might be made as
right as right could be,—yes, the past might
be fully redeemed by the future!

But amidst all her changing hopes and
regrets, she was haunted by a vague sense
of fear, a feeling of which she could not
divest herself, which seemed to tell her that
the blessing she had carelessly thrown away
out of her life might never be recalled,—was
gone for evermore. The soft night-breeze
seemed to be murmuring a sorrowful adieu,
a song of vain regret. In each corner of
the wood, in each shrub and tree, she

seemed to see the face of him in whom
her ideal hero had found his actuality. And
it seemed to her that she was followed always
by large, earnest, sadly reproachful eyes!

The cottage door was reached. Absently
she gave her hand in good-bye to Miles,
while her gaze wandered over and beyond
the wood, as though with the forlorn hope
of seeing him who was far away, out of her
sight. Ten minutes afterwards she might
have found his very self in the wood-land
walk which she had lately felt to be haunted
by his memory.

CHAPTER III.

AFTER escorting Miss Craycroft, with her
friend and other ladies, to their respective
homes, Charles Meredith retraced his steps
with the speed of despairing hope ; and saying to himself, " I must see her once more ;
I cannot rest,—I cannot arrange my thoughts
and form my plans, and learn to bear this
blow,—until I have looked at her again," he
made his way to the wood. Ah, that he might
find her lingering with her fancies, in the
soft air of the summer night! Stay! There
is a gentle rustle! His heart beats fast as
he rounds a corner in the winding path.
He pauses for a moment, and then,—a
quick step brings him face to face with
Miles Grantham, who, pipe in mouth and
slowly sauntering, was brooding darkly, and
thinking cunning thoughts.

Charles' heart gave a great sigh, which none but himself could hear, while with an imperturbable face he greeted Miles. He had hoped to meet the person whom he loved best in all the world. He had encountered, instead, the man whom, of all he had ever seen, he hated most! " Well, it was his fate! Perhaps it was best! Perhaps Miles was just the person whom at that crisis in his life it was best, it was needful that he should meet! The painful opportunity should not be thrown away!"

And soon the two young men were smoking together, and talking in amicable earnestness. The reticent Charles, who, at the beginning of the conversation, would as soon have thought of flying as of allowing his sacred secret to escape him, soon found himself letting it out to him from whom, of all others, he would most have chosen to hide it! Circumstances, necessity, it seemed, had decreed that so it should be. And good angels, looking on, could not stay his hand, could not prevent his yielding up his heart's best earthly treasure into the keeping of an evil spirit who had power to work it woe.

Meanwhile the two young men who were thus conversing together on matters connected with their dearest interests, themselves formed subjects of thoughtful musing to many of those who had been present at the Grantham dance.

When left alone, Sir John Grantham buried his face in his hands, and bowed his head, and gave himself up to bitter musings over a far-back, painful past; or rather indulged himself in bitter thoughts of that which was for him an ever-ending source of painful regret. He lived over again years of vain longing for a son and heir. He felt once more the delicious moment when it seemed that his hopes were about to be realised. " Two-and-twenty years ago ! " He lived over again a time of absence from his wife. He read again a letter from his sister-in-law, Mrs. Grantham, giving unexpected intelligence. Once more he passed through a hurried journey home, not devoid of anxiety, but chiefly full of delightful hope and excite-

ment, and followed by the breathless instant
of arrival, the welcome news " doing well,"
given, however, in faltering tones and with
mournful looks, which cruelly told a cruel
tale. Again he was seeing the hateful face
of his sister-in-law, from whom he had ever
since felt an unconquerable aversion ! Once
more the bitter moment in which he discovered that his baby-son was dead came
back to him. Again he touched the poor
little wasted face, and the little, little hands !
And again he broke away impatiently from
the affected drawl of his sister-in-law's con-
solatory words, " Better this, dear John,
better this, than that he should have grown
up sickly and diseased ! Better this than to
have lost him later on, when you would have
learnt to love your boy ! " " Learnt to love
him ! " At this moment the baronet's heart
yearned over the lost son for whose birth
he had longed so anxiously, and he almost
groaned aloud, " Two-and-twenty years ! "
An echo through his mind, from Charles
Meredith's words, which had taken him into
the past, now recalled him to the present.

"Ah," he sighed, as he thought of the attractive and noble face of his young friend,—"ah, if *her* son had been like that fine young fellow, instead of the mean young humbug that he is, my loss would not have been so bitter,—would not have been so bitter!"

Very different from her husband's were the regretful musings in which Lady Grantham indulged that night. According to her nightly custom, when her maid had left her, she took out of a chest a ghastly picture of her dead baby, gazed at it, shook her head, sighed, let a tear fall upon it, kissed it, and put it away again, murmuring tenderly, "My little boy! my little boy!" But before long her thoughts were pleasantly resting in the present. She reflected how merciful it was that her childless life had been comforted by so good and affectionate a nephew as Miles Grantham. And then she mused over all his perfections, and thought how pleasant were his frequent visits, and his tender attentions to herself! "Dear Miles," she thought, "he is quite a

son to me!" After which, her mind passed
rapidly over the many blessings of her life.
Her lot certainly had fallen upon pleasant
places. Above all things, there was her
husband's love. Then there was the affection of her many friends; and on this head
came in a pleasing romance. How delightful it would be to help forward the evidently
growing attachment between Miles and her
favourite, Margaret Willoughby. The girl
had good birth, a little fortune, personal
attractions,—everything, in short, that a
Grantham could wish to find. Nothing
could be more satisfactory to all parties.
She could not possibly be making a mistake
in trying to promote so desirable an union!
But what would she have said if she could
have seen within the heart of her favourite
that night?

Fain would Margaret have remained out
amidst the trees and flowers, to dream of
her hopes and joys, and to try to stifle her
fears and her regrets! But her mother's
"My dear, make haste and come to bed,"
was not to be gainsaid, and there was

nothing for it but to hasten over her pre-
parations for bed, and to lie down by her
mother's side, with all the restless excitement which made sleep for her impossible.
Would the night never end? Must the
regrets and the unreasonable fears which
pressed upon her with night-mare-like exaggeration, go on for ever? Would the morning never bring with it relief and hope and
action?

CHAPTER IV.

AFTER disturbed slumberings and wakings
and slumberings again, Margaret awoke at
length, to daylight, and hoping she knew
not what from an early rising, stole from
her mother's side, and was soon wandering
in the garden, feeling for a time nothing
but the enjoyment of pleasant anticipation.
After all, what was there to fear? What
was there not to hope from the events of
the coming day. Visions of a happy meeting, a happy talk, sweet things being said,
explanations being made, matters being
satisfactorily arranged, came over her in a
rush, and left her in a glow of impatience
for the hour which must be already on its
wing, to arrive.

When would he come? Would it be
soon? Would it be before luncheon, or

not until the afternoon? How slowly the
time passed! "Not nine o'clock yet!"
When would it be breakfast time? When
would her mother be down? "Nine at
last!" Why was her mother so slow about
coming down? Supposing Mr. Meredith
should call while they were at breakfast, to
make arrangements for a driving or walking
expedition, and should go away not liking
to disturb them! Oh, why was her mother
so dawdling on this particular morning?

She had worked herself up into a regular
fidget, and at length, in a fever of impatience,
was running quickly up to the dinging-room
window, to see why the prayer-bell did not
ring, when her attention was arrested by
the shriek of a railway whistle.

"How I hate that horrid sound!" she
said, petulantly, putting her hands up to
her ears. "The nine-ten train! How late
mamma is!"

But yet she found herself standing to
listen to the rush of the train, and to watch
until an opening through trees brought the
distant steam-engine into momentary view.

She musingly gazed at the long curling cloud of white steam, as it floated sideways on the morning breeze and disappeared into vapour. And as she did so an imaginary horror seized her mind, the thought of a dreadful possibility, from which she awoke, as from a bad dream, to the pleasant reality of the happy summer's day before her.

The prayer-bell was ringing, and she hastened in doors.

"What a perfect morning, mother!" she exclaimed, as she entered through the open window. "We must certainly get up a pic-nic to-day, or do something pleasant."

"Very well, my dear; I dare say Lady Grantham will chaperon you; but don't speak so loud," replied her mother, leaning languidly back in her chair, and pressing her hand on the top of her head.

Margaret's heart sank. "A headache?" she cried, "oh, mother! on this particular day!" And then reproaching herself for feeling selfish disappointment when her mother was suffering, "Of course we cannot go anywhere to-day," she added. And when prayers and breakfast were over, her thoughts were taken up with her mother's wants.

But after settling Mrs. Willoughby on the sofa in her own room, with salts and *eau-de-cologne*, and all the usual requirements of a nervous headache, every possible occupation for the morning seemed to her to be over. She could not give her attention to a book, she could not work without getting the fidgets, she could not write or draw, and music was out of the question on her mother's account. It seemed to her that she could not breathe unless she went out of doors; but even when there she could not rest, for she was never free from the thought that she might have missed hearing a bell at the hall door, and that if she were not in the drawing-room she might be supposed by the servant to be "not at home." So she spent her morning principally in passing in and out of the drawing-room window; at times her heart beat quickly with expectation, and then again sank down low with disappointment. At length she had given up expectation, and comforting herself with the reflection that the morning was nearly over, and that the afternoon *must* bring with it satisfactory results, she had betaken herself to the wood, and had fallen into a pleasant reverie, when suddenly her ear caught a distant sound of feet scuffling along gravel. And,—yes, surely there was a bell,—was it the front door bell? All her restlessness had returned! Once more she hurried across the lawn and through the drawing-room window. No one was there, but on the table lay a parcel of books and a note.

"The Hon. Mrs. Willoughby, with Charles Meredith's best thanks," read Margaret, taking up the parcel; and the note, also, was directed to Mrs. Willoughby. "Why, he only took the books away with him yesterday," she said to herself, "and he generally brings them back himself! How very odd! What can be the meaning of it? Oh, dear, I wish I might open the note! Dillson," she added, to the manservant who came in to announce luncheon, " was any answer asked for to this note ? "

" No, miss."

" Will you tell Jane I want to speak to her ? "

" Yes, miss."

" Jane," went on Margaret, when the lady's maid appeared, " have you been to mamma lately ? "

" Half an hour ago, miss, she rang for me."

" Oh, then I can go to her," interrupted Margaret.

" No, Miss Margaret, you must not go to her," called out Jane, as Margaret was running off. " Your mamma particularly desired that she might not be disturbed. I took her up a bit of luncheon, and she don't want anything more."

It was too provoking ! Margaret's only resource was to hasten to the Hall, as soon as she had despatched her luncheon, in order to find out whether anything had been heard of her friend.

" Well, my dear, so that strange young

man has disappeared," said Lady Grantham, after words of greeting and so forth, had been exchanged between her and her young friend.

"Who?" returned Margaret, blushing scarlet, in spite of all her efforts to appear unconcerned.

"Have not you heard?" said Lady Grantham, looking hard at her, and continuing, "my dear, forgive me, but I fancy you must know something about it. You did quite right. He is not worthy of you. Besides, I believe he is all but engaged to another young lady. I do not wonder at his hurrying off in this fashion, without so much as coming to wish any of us good-bye!"

"I don't understand you, Lady Grantham," returned Margaret, turning very pale, but speaking in a calm and rather haughty tone of voice. "Of whom are you speaking?"

"Surely, my darling, you have heard that Mr. Meredith has gone?" said Lady Grantham, at length becoming more explicit.

"Miles was with him late last night, and saw him off by the nine o'clock train this morning, and gave us the news at breakfast. He spoke very feelingly. Of course *he* can feel for him better than the rest of us can;" here Lady Grantham gave Margaret a meaning smile. "Dear Miles! You know what a generous creature he is; but even he cannot deny that his friend has behaved very badly."

"Lady Grantham," replied Margaret, warmly, drawing herself up, and speaking with a touch of scorn in her tone, which Lady Grantham might or might not have noticed,—"Lady Grantham, whatever Miles may have taken it into his head to fancy, I am quite sure that he can *know* nothing but what is good of Mr. Meredith."

"My dear," said Lady Grantham, in an exhortatory manner, "you really must not allow yourself to be so easily taken in. It is very amiable; but,—only think if you had been of a more susceptible nature, and if things had been a little different from what they are, what a blighted life yours might

have been now! Miles, as you know, is not
apt to entertain suspicions against any one
without sufficient cause. But to say the
truth, I never thoroughly liked that young
man. He is very pleasant, just the sort of
creature to take a young girl's heart by
storm, but he does not give me the notion
of being steady; and, in short, my dear, I
am sure he is not worthy of any young
woman's regard. What a contrast there is
between him and Miles!"

"Certainly; there could not well be two
people more unlike!" said Margaret, who
was sorely tempted to launch out strongly
on the subject of her companion's nephew,
but contented herself with a contemptuous
smile at his expense. "But surely, Lady
Grantham," she went on, "I have often
heard both you and Sir John praise Mr.
Meredith up to the skies? I thought that
you had taken a great fancy to him. Miles
must——"

The entrance of Miles himself cut off the
remainder of her speech.

"What is it that Miles must do?" he

asked, in his affected drawl, as he squeezed
her unwilling hand, and half raised to
hers, and then self-consciously lowered, his
cowardly eyes, just avoiding the sight of
the contemptuous curl of her lip with which
she returned his greeting.

"I was just telling Margaret about Mr.
Meredith's sudden departure. I believe she
thinks that you are rather hard upon him,"
said Lady Grantham.

"Hard upon him! Indeed, Margaret, it
is *you* who are hard upon *me!* Hard upon
him! I am awfully sorry for him, I can
assure you. *I* ought to be the last person
to blame him too severely."

Margaret could have knocked him down
as he spoke.

"He consulted me, and I hope I gave
him good advice; for his own sake I-thought
he was right to go."

"Where is he gone to?" asked Margaret,
unconcernedly, wilfully misunderstanding the
words of Miles' mysterious whisper. "I
suppose he means to return?"

"N—o, I.—I fancy not," answered Miles,

somewhat taken aback by her manner.
" He is going up to town for a day or two,
I believe, and after that I don't know
what his plans may be. Perhaps he will
write."

"Perhaps so," returned Margaret. "Good-
bye, Lady Grantham ; I must go home and
see how mamma is. Good-bye, Miles."

" Could not you and your mother come
in quietly this evening ?" called out Lady
Grantham after her, as she was making her
escape through the window.

" Thanks, Lady Grantham ; but I am
afraid mamma will not be up to it," answered Margaret, running off, wilfully heed-
less that Miles had intended to accompany
her home.

She found Mrs. Willoughby in the drawing-room, and almost well again.

" So you have been to the Hall, my
dear ?" she said, with a smile, as Margaret
appeared.

" Yes, mother. Have you found your
note ?"

" From Mr. Meredith ? Yes. You have

heard, I suppose, that he has left? It is a very sudden change of plan!"

"Does he give any reason?" asked Margaret.

Her mother gave her the note. "Grateful and civil," she said, as she watched Margaret's eyes pass quickly over the sheet, "but mysterious, to say the least of it."

Margaret was silent, and her mother was puzzled by the expression of her face as she kept it bent over the letter, reading again and again to herself the words, "Pray believe that I shall never forget the great kindness which you and your daughter have shown to me during the happy weeks that I have spent in your neighbourhood."

"Fancy his going off in this sudden manner!" went on Mrs. Willoughby. "There is something nice about the boy. He is pleasant, but not very interesting. I should not say that he had a vast amount of brain."

"Mother, his going is all Miles' doing," said Margaret, suddenly looking up.

"Miles' doing! What in the world do

you mean, my dear? What could Miles have to do with his going?"

"Oh mother, mother, help me!" cried Margaret, all her reserve breaking down in a moment, while all the meaning of her trouble came over her. And kneeling down by her mother, she leaned her head upon her lap, and sobbed as if her heart would break.

"My child, my child, what is it?" said Mrs. Willoughby, soothingly.

And when she was calm enough to speak, Margaret told her mother all the story of her joy and grief.

"Oh, mother, do you think he will come back again?" she said. "Do you think that I shall ever be able to explain to him, —to let him know that,—that,— Oh, mother, I was so unkind, so cruel! Oh, how could I be so blind and stupid!" And getting quickly up from her knees, she clasped her hands together in an agony of unavailing regret.

"My darling! my darling! it will be all right, if you will only believe it. Indeed, you are distressing yourself unnecessarily," her mother said, caressingly.

"Do you really think it will be all right, mother?" asked Margaret, eagerly. "Do tell me what we can do?"

"I will think it over, my love; and meanwhile you must be patient, and remember that you have nothing with which to reproach yourself. In a few days you may feel very differently from what you do now. You are excited to-day, and do not understand your own feelings."

Margaret's heart sank. This was not the sort of comfort that she wanted. "What do you mean, mamma?" she said, sadly.

"I mean, dear child, that I think you are giving way to fanciful and morbid regrets. You liked Mr. Meredith, and were pleased at his liking you. You are sorry for him, and now that he is out of your reach you begin to dream that you return his affection."

A storm of passion seemed to take possession of Margaret while her mother's words came out in slow and measured tones. She only looked her answer. She could not speak, but her face expressed something of the pain, wonderment, and consternation that she was feeling.

"And probably," went on Mrs. Willough-by, "you exaggerate, also, the strength of his feeling for you. You may be mistaking a mere passing fancy for love, and——"

"Mother!" burst in Margaret, at length, "how little you know, how little you understand!"

"My dear child," said her mother, "I know and understand well enough! I can sympathize with you perhaps better than you think. I had my own dreams and fancies when I was a girl like you; and when I was about your age I think I must have been very much in your present state of mind. I fancied myself in love with some one who paid me great attentions, but by-and-by it turned out that he had been flirting with another girl all the time, and then I discovered the worth of the man who really cared for me."

Mrs. Willoughby spoke in measured tones,

and it seemed to Margaret as if she were slowly and indifferently reading her thoughts out of a book. All the more she felt how little her mother was understanding her actual trouble and difficulty.

"Well, mamma," she answered, this time speaking quietly enough, "at all events it was not a man like Miles Grantham who cared, or *could* care, about you really; and I do not quite see that your case was very like mine."

"My dear," returned her mother, "I cannot bear to hear you speak of Miles in the tone that you do. It is mere perversity, because you know how much he loves you, and how much our hearts are set on your——"

"Mother," broke in Margaret, impetuously, "don't say it! please, don't say it! You know—you know quite well that it would be utterly impossible for me to take to Miles!" She paused, too breathless with agitation to say more; and her mother, seeing her face of disgust, felt that she had been imprudent, and added more kindly,—

"Well, well, my love, we will not say

anything more about it now. I only want
you to try to conquer your prejudice against
poor Miles. It can be nothing but a blind
prejudice which keeps you from appreciating
his excellence. Of course, my dear, I do
not pretend to know how strong Mr. Meredith's feeling for you may be, so you need
not let anything that I have said disturb
you. It is only that I do not want you to
mourn over spilt milk!"

"Mamma, I only said what I did say
because I thought you might be able to help
me. I see that you cannot, so please we
will not talk any more on the subject. I
will try to be patient, as you tell me; but it
is very hard when one feels that things
might have been all right, but for one's own
fault, and when one is sure that one has
made another person unhappy and can
think of no way of undoing the mischief."

"My love, do not you suppose that Mr.
Meredith could make it all right, as you say,
if he chose? When a man is very eager in
his love he is not in such a hurry to give up
trying to win the girl he loves. And besides,

men are not so slow as you seem to imagine about discovering when they are loved, and——"

At this moment came a knock at the drawing-room door, and Miles Grantham entered.

"At any rate," thought Margaret to herself, "some men are slow enough about discovering when they are hated!"

"I am come to see how you are, Mrs. Willoughby?" said Miles. "My aunt cannot quite give up the hope that you may be well enough to give us the pleasure of your company this evening; Margaret will have told you——"

"No, mother," interrupted Margaret, quickly; I forgot to give Lady Grantham's kind message; but as you had just said that you should keep quiet all day, and not go out at all——"

"Ah, but I shall be quite well enough to come to the Hall this evening," broke in Mrs. Willoughby, eagerly. "Pray thank your aunt, and tell her that we shall be very happy to look in."

"I really cannot go, mamma," said Margaret, when Miles had left them to themselves again. But poor Margaret found herself obliged to submit, not only to the visit, but to more love-making on the part of Miles than she had yet had to endure. It was just such an evening as the previous one had been. Lady Grantham proposed a moonlight stroll in the grounds, and insisted upon it that the "young people" should not adapt themselves to her own and Mrs. Willoughby's pace. And once more Margaret found herself wandering, against her will, with one companion, across lawns, by shrubberies, and through pleasant glades. Once more her favourite wood became the scene of a *tête-à-tête* walk; and once more she was listening to a young man's professions of love and of admiration. Would it have been possible for Miles to understand the torture that he was inflicting on his companion as they walked side by side near the wooded glen,—that glen, which, as long as Margaret could remember, had been to her a happy world, peopled by imaginary beings, and which now had become haunted, for her, by remembrances, both blissful and regretful, connected with her own actual life? Under any circumstances, to be kept prisoner by the man she hated, to have to listen to the affected softness of his voice, and to his twaddling sentiments, would have been trying enough; but to have added to this those "happier things" of that evening gone by, pressing upon her memory, made the infliction seem almost more than she could bear.

Would it never end? Must the nightmare last for evermore?

Hark! Was not that the blessed sound of an approaching footstep, giving the joyful promise of relief at hand? Was not that the delightful sound of a gentleman clearing his throat?

Yes! Another moment brought them face to face with Sir John Grantham! and the *tête-à-tête* was put an end to just in time to avoid the answering of an awkwardly-put question.

"Beg pardon," said Sir John, making as

though to pass by; I did not mean to be guilty of interrupting a *tête-à-tête.*"

"Oh, I am so glad we have met you," cried Margaret, eagerly. "I have hardly spoken to you all the evening, and Miles and I are so stupid to-night, that I think we should have had to murder each other for the sake of a little excitement, if you had not suddenly appeared on the scene.

"Ah, we want poor Charlie Meredith to enliven us!" cried Sir John, as he turned and began walking, with his hand on his darling's shoulder, and looked searchingly into her blushing face.

"Yes, you will miss him, Sir John," she answered, with affected carelessness, "and so shall we all. Why did he go off in such a hurry?"

"I thought you and Miles knew all about that," returned Sir John. "He seemed out of spirits last night, and hinted that it might be necessary for him to run away sooner than he had intended; but I did not know that he was speaking quite in such sober earnest."

"He would have been a scoundrel if he

remained any longer!" put in Miles, and his self-conscious face bore a black and evil expression as he spoke.

"Miles' talent for enigma grows!" cried Margaret, with a forced laugh. "He might have taken a first-class degree in that accomplishment, if in nothing else! Oh, don't let us turn up by the lawn yet. It is too fine to go in. You and I must have a *tête-à-tête* walk now, dear Sir John," she said, looking coaxingly up into his face, and without paying any attention to Miles' die-away looks, she dragged her old friend along the way she chose to go, according to an old established custom against which he would have found it useless to rebel.

In fact, ever since she was a toddling child of two years old Margaret had had pretty much her own way with Sir John Grantham, and had been allowed to tyrannise over him and plague him, to her heart's content, getting nothing worse than caresses and petting in return for all her coercion and tyranny.

"Well, what have you got to say to me

now you have got me, childie? It is a little
hard,—is not it,—to have *chasé-ed* poor Miles
in that off-hand manner?" he said, now with
very gentle reproach.

"Indeed, sometimes I wish I could *chasser*
him altogether," returned Margaret. "Oh,
if you could know what a tease and nuisance,
—forgive me, I ought not to have said this
to you, dear Sir John, when he is your
nephew."

Sir John was looking very grave. He
turned away to smother a sigh, and then,
"My dear, I think you *are* hard upon
Miles," he said. "I believe I am hard
upon him myself sometimes. But I know,
from what my wife says, how really good
and worthy he is! And you and I must try
to understand him better. We must not
allow ourselves to be prejudiced by little
peculiarities of manner. We must not forget that it is not always the most attractive
people who make the most desirable friends.
That young Meredith is a taking fellow
enough, but he may be very wild."

Sir John was not like himself! Margaret

had never heard him speak in such a prim
and tiresome way before! What in the
world did he mean? Miles must have got
hold of him and made him believe something false. And yet he hated Miles as
much as she did, of this Margaret was sure.
What did it mean? Poor Margaret! It
meant that on one point, and that a vital
point, she was not to have her own way,
even with her indulgent old friend Sir John
Grantham. It meant that even he was unit-
ing with the other conspirators who, unknown
to her, in their very love and kindness, were
plotting against her future peace and happiness. In short, Sir John Grantham was as
much bent as his wife upon having Margaret as a niece, adopted daughter, and
the mistress elect of Grantham Hall. He
sighed over the thought that so charming a
creature should be thrown away on one so
unworthy of her, but he could not relinquish
his favourite scheme, which had been growing in his mind with the growth of Margaret's years; and there was nothing for
it but to try to deceive himself into the

belief that Miles was a very good fellow,
and that only his own power of appreciation
was at fault. His wife, a paragon of perfection in his eyes, must surely be a better
judge of character than himself: and was
not she devoted to the heir apparent of
Grantham Hall? He had heard something
of the state of affairs connected with Charles
and Margaret, and suspected more than he
had heard. And it was not without a touch
of remorseful regret that he reflected on
what would have made so pretty an union.
But he set himself sedulously to crush the
foolish piece of sentiment out of his heart.
"Ah, he is a pleasant young fellow!" he
thought. "Better that they should not see
too much of each other. It would never
do! A younger son. Not sufficient means.
Wild and extravagant; probably not of any
family. Who knows what these Merediths
may be? Would not do at all!"

"Have you any reason to suppose that
he is 'wild'?" asked Margaret, presently.
"I thought that you had a very high opinion
of him."

"High opinion? I know nothing about him, my dear. We all agreed in enjoying his society, and we shall all agree in missing him exceedingly. I confess I don't quite understand his running away in such a hurry. If he cares very much about us, and has a clear conscience, perhaps he will turn up again some day. Meanwhile, I believe the less some of us think of him the better. Better to make the best of what we have than to dream of that which is out of our reach, and which ·we, perhaps, should not like if we could have it. Eh, childie?"

Margaret had begun the *tête-à-tête* with some vague intention of becoming confidential, with some vague hope of being helped out of her troubles. But her intentions had been frozen by the unwonted chilliness of Sir John's manner, and her hopes faded away. They were "all alike!" she thought. She must bear her burden alone; the burden which it was hard to bear, because it contained the burden of another person's sorrow caused by herself. Certainly she would not have been encouraged had she overheard the conversation that had taken place between her mother and Lady Grantham, who, on being left to each other's society, had eagerly begun discussing " the event of the day."

" I am afraid the poor child is a little bit fascinated," said Lady Grantham, in the course of conversation.

" Yes, but she will soon get over that," returned Mrs. Willoughby. " It would not do at all. He is a very good-natured young man, but not at all the sort of person I should choose Margaret to marry."

" No, indeed ; and if you had heard Miles talk you would think so all the more. You know how kind-hearted dear Miles is. He would not hurt a fly, dear fellow, much less slander a neighbour. He said all he could for Mr. Meredith, but it is impossible not to see what his real opinion is. And, of course, for that dear child's sake, he could not be altogether silent. My dear Mrs. Willoughby, what a treasure she has in his heart! and he could not have made a better choice."

"No," sighed Mrs. Willoughby, "if only——"

"But you must be firm with the dear child, my dear," interrupted Lady Grantham, quickly. "She must conquer her romantic fancy, and learn to find out what is for her true happiness."

"She is a dear unselfish girl. I am sure she will consider our feelings," said Mrs. Willoughby, in her slow, languid tones; "but I am afraid I shall have rather a battle with her. I wish that tiresome young man had never come in her way! A younger son, extravagant, and—oh, it is out of the question!"

"But you don't imagine that there is any doubt of her being really attached to Miles?" returned Lady Grantham, in rather a stiff and aggrieved manner.

"At the bottom of her heart, I am convinced that she loves him. How could she help it?" said Mrs. Willoughby. "But you know young girls are so foolish,—so fond of dreaming of the absent! When I was a girl——"

"My dear," impatiently interrupted Lady Grantham, "she must hear nothing about the young man. She must not so much as see his name in the newspaper. We must never talk of him. If the flame is not fed, it must die out by degrees."

"What is that about feeding the flames? Good heavens! You don't mean to say you have been lighting the fire this sultry night!" cried Sir John Grantham, coming quickly into the drawing-room, where the ladies were now seated, and, by his loud laugh and pretended exclamation of horror, trying "to get up the steam," as he would have expressed it, after his embarrassing and depressing conversation with Margaret.

And thus plotting and persecution for the time being were brought to an end.

CHAPTER V.

WHEN Margaret awoke the next morning, she had no inclination such as she had felt on the previous one, to hurry up and out of doors. There was nothing to be ready for, no joy to reach after, no opportunity to arrive for making straight that which had been made crooked, nothing to come !— nothing but a weary day of regret before her ! With a great pain at her heart, which seemed to strike freshly from time to time, she mused wonderingly over the change which the last few days had brought into her life. Was it possible that so short a time could have passed since that morning when she had last awakened to the old state of things, to life in that Dreamland which would have been the perfection of happiness if it could only have become a reality ?

Was it only the day before yesterday that
she had gone about so happily and carelessly ignorant of the great flash of light
that was coming to meet her, and of the
shadow with which she herself was to over-
cast the unexpected light? Could it have
been only two nights since this had happened,
—since she who loved him had darkened *his*
life? Could it have been only the morning
of the day before that she had been so full
of hope and of anxiety? It seemed as if in
the short space of time she had lived the
life of two long ages, and that now there
was nothing more to come! And yet life
had grown so much richer, so infinitely
dearer, that she would not for the world
have gone back to what it had been before
it had shown her that she loved him!
"Nothing more to come!" Yes, so it
seemed, for there was nothing that she
could do, there was no one who could help
her, every one was against her, no one
cared for him! There was nothing for it
but to wait. She must learn to be patient.
As she resigned herself, however, to this

thought, and made her resolution of patience, hope began unawares to spring up again in her heart. It was possible, at least, that a letter might come from Mr. Meredith that very day, to Lady Grantham or to her mother. It was even possible that he might change his mind and return! In short, a thousand hopeful possibilities began to shape themselves in her imagination. But then there was Miles!—Miles, who was always ready to work mischief and spoil sport. And at the recollection of Miles, the cunning kill-joy, her heart sank again, and muttering to herself, " He *shall not* have it all his own way, and make everybody miserable," she jumped out of bed, all her patience and resignation changed into very impatient restlessness.

She was certain of Charles Meredith's love, her faith in it had not been in the least degree shaken by the chilling words of her mother and her friends; but she determined for the future to keep her treasure to herself. No one should see how much she cared. She would ask for news of Mr.

Meredith in an unconcerned and natural manner, and Sir John Grantham should be made to feel that Miles was not to be trusted, and that Mr. Meredith was deserving of all faith and confidence.

"Oh, dear, how I wish that the morning was over!" sighed Margaret, walking towards the window, after a glance at the breakfast table, where lay what she considered an uninteresting set of letters for her mother. "How tiresome and stupid everything looks and seems! What can I do until it is time for me to go to Grantham Hall, to see——"

"My dear child, what is the matter? What are you grumbling about?"

Mrs. Willoughby had entered unperceived by Margaret, who turned round quickly, startled and annoyed by her mother's languidly-spoken interruption to her soliloquy.

"No letters, that is all," she answered, brusquely. "A headache again, mother?"

"My dear, you know I always have one, more or less," returned her mother, with a sigh. "I wish you would learn to be a little more gentle."

"Why *can't* the doctors cure you?" impatiently exclaimed Margaret, almost thankful for something on which to vent her irritation.

"Ah, they will never do that," returned Mrs. Willoughby, resignedly. "Never mind me, my dear. For your sake, though, I wish I had my health! If I were only up to travelling, we might have carried out Lady Grantham's pleasant little proposal. She and Miles had been agreeing that a trip abroad would do you good, and I believe it was Miles' suggestion that he should be our escort on the continent."

"Very charming!" cried Margaret; "and then we might top up with a lunatic asylum, where we might dream perpetually that we were still gazing at snow mountains in Miles Grantham's sweet society!"

"Don't be silly, Margaret," returned her mother. "You are very wrong and ungrateful! You little know all that you have to thank Miles for."

"I do indeed little know all that I have to thank Miles for!" thought Margaret,

bitterly, to herself, but aloud she said,
"Well, but, mother, as you are not up to
the carrying out of this delightful scheme,
it is perhaps as well that my inclinations
do not lean that way." And so she deftly
changed the topic of conversation to one
almost equally interesting to Mrs. Willoughby, viz., that of her own poor
health.

Then followed a weary morning! Having settled her mother on the sofa, and
preformed her various errands, she seated
herself with a book, which, however, for the
most part, lay idly on her knee, while her
thoughts strayed far away. If she might
only have been left to the luxury of her sad
or restless musings, without the disturbing
influence of her mother's continually recur-
ring glance, they would have been easier
to bear. But to have to feel Mrs. Wil--
loughby's eyes fixed curiously upon her,
from time to time, was almost more, it
seemed, than flesh and blood could endure.

"My dear, you seem to be very idle to
day, I wish you would try to rouse yourself,"

said her mother, presently, languidly looking off from her crochet work.

It was not Mrs. Willoughby's wont to trouble herself much as to whether Margaret was industrious or not,—why should she have done so on this particular morning? Margaret knit her brows, tried to stifle a feeling of irritation, and once more took up her book, but soon she involuntarily let it fall again on her lap.

" My dear Margaret, I wish you would get something to do! I don't like to see you wasting your time in this way," said her mother, presently.

" I was reading," returned Margaret, rising quickly from her seat and putting her book upon the table. " But I believe it is too hot to do anything. I am lazy, somehow. Shall I go and talk to Gilling, mother, about those rose-buddings that you want him to get from the Hall gardener? "

The rose-buddings were a happy notion, and she went out into the August sunshine, saying to herself, " What a fool I was ! What a fool I was ! What a happy day this might have been! How happy *he* might have been! And now,—and now!"

Thus sighing, she made her way to the garden, where she found old Gilling standing, in meditative mood, and with an expression of such gloom on his face as might have been caused by a reflection from her own thoughts.

"Gilling!" she called, "Gilling!" and he started as if he had been surprised in the performance of some guilty deed.

"Why, Miss Marget, how sudden you do come down upon a body, to be sure!" and Margaret laughed merrily at his discomfiture.

"What is the matter, Gilling?" she asked. "Are all the rose-trees dying? or have you been committing murder or theft?"

"Matter? What should be the matter, Miss Marget?" returned the old man, testily. "Thank heaven my conscience is clear as to the eighth commandment and the sixth, too, and, for the matter of that, I can't see but what I've kept all the commandments reg'lar all my life."

" And how is your wife, Gilling ? "

" Terrible low and bad, to be sure. You haven't been to see her lately, Miss Marget."

" No," answered Margaret, her heart smiting her; "yesterday, I—I don't know how it has happened. I'll go this afternoon."

" She'll be terribly glad to see you. She've been talking of you a deal. And what's gone so sudden with that young gentleman what was down here, Miss Marget ? " asked old Gilling, abruptly, while he turned his inquisitive glance straight upon poor Margaret's disconcerted countenance.

"I can't tell you, Gilling," she replied, with an embarrassed laugh. " I suppose he was not able to stay here any longer."

" I suppose he'll be coming back again ? "

" I don't know, indeed. Scarcely likely, I should fancy."

" He's a nice spoken gentleman. My old woman thinks a deal of him, says as Mr. Miles ain't fit to hold a candle to him. But I ain't going to have nothing said agen Mr. Miles. He's been a good friend to me, and——"

" By-the-by, that reminds me, Gilling,"
interrupted Margaret, " mamma wished me
to speak to you about the rose-buddings."

" Oh, yes, miss.; I'll go over to the Hall.
Here comes Mr. Miles ! You must be quick
if you want to hide from him, Miss Marget,"
whispered the old man, with a wink.

Many a time, in her childhood, had he
helped Margaret to find a hiding-place from
the teasing search of her tyrannical playfellow, Miles. And never in her childhood
would she so gladly have hailed a refuge
from her tormentor as at this present moment.
But alas, she had been seen ! She could not
with any degree of decency make her escape,
and Mr. Miles, the grown gentleman, might
not be treated so unceremoniously by the old
gardener as Master Miles, the schoolboy,
had been treated in days of old.

" Margaret," said Miles, coming close up
to her, " Mrs. Willoughby sent me to look
for you. I have come to ask you if you
will ride with me this afternoon."

" Thanks, but I have an engagement, and
cannot possibly ride," returned Margaret.

Of course, however, all Margaret's objections were overruled by her mother, and of course she was obliged to say that she would go.

" Margaret," said Miles, when conversasion seemed to be flagging, during the course of the afternoon ride, " I heard from Meredith this morning. He desires his kindest regards to everybody, and especially to you and your mother.

" Really ! " returned Margaret.

" Perhaps," said Miles, in a would-be tender and pathetic tone, which nevertheless affected Margaret's mind somewhat in the like manner as she might have been affected physically by a polar wind in spring, " perhaps you would have preferred a warmer message ! "

" I would prefer, if you please," answered Margaret, " to talk of something else."

" But I," said Miles, " choose that you should listen to me. Margaret, you shall trifle with me no longer——"

" Trifle ! " echoed Margaret, with a glance of haughty astonishment. " Trifle ? What

do you mean ? Do you mean anything,
or——"

"I mean, Margaret," returned Miles,
theatrically, "I mean, in all sober earnestness, that I will be satisfied, once for all, as to
whether you have been playing with me all
this time, whether each look or word, which I
have innocently interpreted to signify devotion such as that which I feel for you,
whether each apparent sign of love has been
a mere mockery,—a mere pretence, such as
that which Charles Meredith showed to you
and you to him,—or——"

"Be silent, Mr. Grantham," exclaimed
Margaret, in a tone of suppressed passion.
"Dare to say another word such as those which
you have just spoken, and, and—" Here her
dignity broke down, she was breathless from
the effect of the excessive excitement which
she was trying to control, and no threat that
would not have appeared ludicrously ineffec-
tive was forthcoming from her mind at the
right moment. She paused, irresolute and
panting.

"Margaret," went on Miles, "I never

suspected you of flirting until I saw you
with——"

"Stay!—stop!" cried Margaret, interrupt-
her companion with startling promptitude.
"Do you hear? I will not listen to another
word. Sir John Grantham shall know of this,
and, and——"

"Margaret, it is true," burst in Miles, with
desperate determination. A frightful possibility had crossed his cowardly mind while
Margaret was speaking; but thinking his
wisest course would be to take the bull by
the horns, he made an effort to hide his
fears under a manner of vehement assurance.
"Margaret, it is true!" he cried. "Till
Meredith came, till I watched your behaviour
with him, I understood your manner to me
to mean the love that it expressed. Am I
now to understand that you have been
deceiving me,—that you only gave me
encouragement in order that you might
have the satisfaction of trampling my heart
as a worm beneath your feet?"

"Deceiving you! Gave you encouragement!" returned Margaret, this

time with calm and contemptuous indignation. " Trampling *your* heart ! " | Here her sense of the ludicrous almost conquered dignity and anger; but she would not allow her lips to curl even into a smile of contempt. " Mr. Grantham," she continued, with dignified gravity, " you know well enough, you cannot deny that you know, that I have given you no encouragement, that I have not even believed in your pretended affection, that I have escaped from you and your unwelcome attentions whenever I have found it possible, that I have hated you almost as long as I can remember, and have borne with your companionship only for the sake of my friends, Sir John and Lady Grantham, whom I love so well, and to whom I owe so much."

" You have not believed in my affection ! " exclaimed Miles, working himself up into a fervour of theatrical passion. " By heaven, then you shall believe in it soon ! You shall feel it as a powerful force, subduing your hatred, making you love me, whether you will or no ! Margaret, you *shall* love

me, or if you will not love me, still, you
shall be mine! Every one desires it,—my
uncle, my aunt, your mother,—and nothing
but your own perversity, and your fancy for
a man who does not love you,—for all he
found it pleasant to amuse himself with you
during a summer holiday,—could keep you
from desiring it too."

Here Margaret's sense of the ludicrous
was irresistibly touched by Miles Grantham's
cool and impertinent conceit. She burst
out laughing, and then,—

"In short," she replied, "no right-
minded young woman to whom Miles
Grantham should condescend to recommend
himself could fail to perceive the eligibility
of the offer! And you really think," she
went on, changing her tone, "that when my
mother and Sir John and Lady Grantham
hear of your conduct to me to day they will
still wish——"

"Margaret!" interrupted Miles. He
felt that he had gone too far, and this time
the intonation of his voice was humbly
despairing. "Margaret, forgive me! You

little know how much I love you, how
worthy of all honour I deem you to be."

("I believe he fancies that he is in a
book!" thought Margaret to herself.)

"Perhaps some day" he went on "you
will better understand my devotion, and will
learn to think more kindly of me! Meanwhile, let this conversation remain a secret
between you and me?" He spoke imploringly, for fear and vanity were working
busily within him.

"Stop a moment," returned Margaret;
"this must depend entirely upon yourself.
Will you promise never again to talk to me
on the subject of which you have spoken to
day?—never again to speak or look at me
in a way which you mean to express nonsense? In that case, I will keep your
secret; otherwise, in self-defence, I must
tell Sir John of all that has passed to-day."

"Margaret," he said, "you are hard
upon me,—you are cruel! How can I
promise what you ask? I will promise this
much, and no more. I will promise that my
love shall not annoy you again during the

remainder of my visit at Grantham ; and, after that, who knows how long it may be before we meet again ? It may be a year or more before I return to Grantham ; but through all that time my heart will remain staunch to you, and I shall not relinquish the hope of conquering your cruel repugnance to me ! "

"You can please yourself, as to that," replied Margaret. "Meanwhile, your secret shall be safe with me, until you cause me to repent my indulgence." She gave her answer lightly, while her heart bounded gladly at the prospect of a year's freedom from persecution. What joys might not that year bring forth !

Miles, also, softly heaved a sigh of relief. He was safe!—for Margaret would not break her word, and, despite her want of appreciation, he would quietly work his way, and win the prize yet. His vanity told him it was impossible she could withstand him to the end ; and he had her mother on his side. Yes, with the aid of Mrs. Willoughby and his aunt, whom he had almost entirely

under his thumb, he should surely succeed!
Besides, hitherto Margaret had not believed
in his devotion to her; now he would teach
her at the same time to believe in it, and to
disbelieve in that of Charles Meredith !

CHAPTER VI.

WHEN Margaret arrived at home, she found Lady Grantham and her mother seated together beneath a tree on the lawn.

" Back already, child!" cried Lady Grantham, looking at her watch. " Just dinner-time ! I had no idea it was so late. Good-bye, my dear Mrs. Willoughby. Margaret, I have scarcely set eyes on you to-day! Walk with me as far as the avenue. Well, and did you enjoy your ride ? "

" Oh yes, thanks," replied Margaret, quickly. " That is to say, it was pleasant in the pine wood, otherwise it was a little bit hot."

At the tone of Margaret's answer, Lady Grantham's heart sank. She had hoped for great results from this ride.

" Which way did you go ? " she asked.

"Oh, past the scene of our last week's picnic. You have not heard from Mr. Meredith, I suppose, Lady Grantham?"

"Miles heard this morning," was the answer.

"Oh!" said Margaret, as though the information had been new, and then each silently pursued her opposite thoughts.

"Well, my love, did you enjoy your ride?" was asked again, when Margaret rejoined her mother.

"Oh, it was so awfully hot, mother," answered Margaret. "What have you been doing? Had any visitors?"

"No one but Alice Craycroft and Lady Grantham. But I want to hear about your ride," said her mother, rather querulously.

"I wish Alice Craycroft had been in my place!" returned Margaret, laughing.

"Nonsense, Margaret; I am sure by your face that you have something to tell me! Has he spoken?"

"Mamma, please don't let us talk of Miles," said Margaret, quickly. "I have really nothing to tell you."

" You have refused him, I am sure you have refused him ! Margaret, you will break my heart ! " Here Mrs. Willoughby subsided into a fit of hysterics, which perhaps may have spared her daughter the pain of witnessing the catastrophe of the threatened broken heart !

For a while Margaret was engrossed in restoring and soothing her mother. Then fell night, to be followed by another weary restless morning ! Mrs. Willoughby was laid up with one of her worst headaches, and accused her child of having caused it by her wilfulness and want of sympathy ; and Margaret was one moment lovingly remorseful, and the next impatiently annoyed by her mother's querulous and unjust complaints. And her heart aching doubly from the sense of lack of sympathy, she again strove in vain to find any occupation which would divert her mind from her trouble.

She could not get rid of the impression that evil was being worked behind her back, and found herself constantly oppressed by the restless sensation that there must be

something which she might be doing to
counteract its effects. Oh, for some one to
help her! Oh, for some light to fall upon
the dreary darkness! She thought, like
many a young girl before her, that no lot
could be more wretched than hers. And
then, to prove the falsity of this thought,
came, from no apparent cause, the re-action
of a great flood of joy and hope! After all,
her memories were glad enough to make
her hopeful! She went to the Hall, in full
expectation of hearing that Sir John and
Lady Grantham had received a letter from
Mr. Meredith, restoring him to their good
graces again.

"I suppose you have not heard from Mr.
Meredith, Lady Grantham?" once more
she asked, apparently in the most accidental and unconcerned manner.

"Miles heard yesterday," was this time
Lady Grantham's answer. And then a
dose composed of Miles' charms was
poured down Margaret's throat, and again
old Nurse Gilling was to be done out of a
visit from her darling, because the morning

ended in arrangements for an afternoon expedition, and Margaret was not allowed to escape the pleasure provided for her.

Miles made his appearance, looking like a beaten dog; and his manner towards Margaret was deprecating and mournful. Whenever he approached her, his movements appeared to be asking pardon for the liberty they were taking. He oppressed her all the afternoon with small attentions, in a way which seemed to be saying, "You may crush me, you may despise and hate me, but you cannot prevent my serving you!" And the sensation that he effected in her was an intense desire to crush him, as if he had been a loathsome insect. But as, unfortunately, this desirable object might not and could not be obtained, she had to endure the same kind of irritating persecution daily, during the remainder of Miles' visit at Grantham!

A day or two passed, and then Margaret said again,—

"Have you had any news from Mr. Meredith, by-the-by, Lady Grantham?"

"Miles heard on Thursday," replied Lady Grantham.

"What is that?" asked Sir John, looking up from a book of which he was turning over the leaves, and catching sight of the weary, wistful face which Margaret had hastily turned away from Lady Grantham's view. "What is that? And you heard too, did not you, old woman? Surely you saw the letter, childie? it was full of pleasant reminiscences of the Hall and of The Cottage. You were meant to see it, I'll be bound."

"My dear, it was only a line, thanking for favours received," said Lady Grantham, laughing. "If I had supposed that it would have been any gratification to Margaret to see the interesting document, you may be sure I should not have forgotten to show it to her. Miles' was the principal letter. He read us parts of it, you know."

"Have you destroyed your note?" asked Sir John, who was suddenly possessed by an impression that between them they were bullying the girl, in a way that he could not permit.

"Oh no, I think not," said Lady Grantham, feeling in her pocket. "I gave it to you, I believe, and I have not seen it since. Most likely you were the destroyer."

"That I am sure I was not," returned her husband. "Oh, ay; here it is, safe in my waistcoat pocket!" and he held it out to Margaret.

It contained little more than what she had already gathered from Sir John Grantham. But there was something in the actual wording, and in the sight of the handwriting, that seemed to bring her comfort. She felt, after reading the letter, as if he were not so far away, and it seemed as though her future meeting with him had become a nearer possibility.

"When you write to him, will you be so kind as to thank him for his note to mamma? And will you tell him that we were very sorry he was obliged to run away in such a hurry, and that we did not see him to say good-bye? Mamma says it is not worth while her writing in return for that note. Writing tires her head," said Margaret, adding, sigh-ingly, to herself, " I wish she would let me write for her. And yet, and yet—I don't know that I should dare to do it, even if she would ! "

" My dear," replied Lady Grantham, " I put a line into Miles' envelope on Thursday. I always like to answer my letters at once."

In spite of herself, Margaret flushed with vexation.

" Too bad, childie," said the Squire. " You and I knew nothing about it, and were never asked for messages. I'll tell you what, I'll write myself by this very day's post, and you shall send what message you like."

" I'll be hanged if that young prig shall have it all his own way," he added, to himself, as he caught sight of Miles, approaching the group on the terrace walk. " We shall be having the poor child going off into a decline, and lose her altogether, which would be worse than losing her from Grantham Hall ! I say, Miles,"—aloud, when his nephew had come up,—" will this same address still find young Meredith ? "

" I—I don't know, uncle," answered

Miles. "Are you going to write to him? Perhaps it would be better to wait until I have heard again?"

" Oh, nonsense! of course the letter would be forwarded."

" Oh, no doubt," returned Miles, suddenly changing his tone.

" I must be quick, though," said Sir John, looking at his watch; " it is nearly time for the letters to go."

" I am going down to Darlingster by-and-by, uncle, and can post any letters, if you like. So you need not hurry," called out Miles, as his uncle left the terrace.

" All right, thank you," said the squire, adding to himself, " I'll be hanged if he shall take this one, though, with those lank, ill-favoured claws of his."

The letter was written,—a genial, hearty letter, expressing the general regret at Charles' hasty departure, recommending as speedy a return, and hinting pretty clearly that his society had not been found dis-agreeable to the inmates of The Cottage. Having completed, folded, and directed it,

Sir John rang the bell, and hearing that
the bag had already gone, gave orders that
one of the men should take his letter into
Darlingster.

It would have been as much as the foot-
man's place was worth if Sir John had known
that he had given up the letter to Miles, who,
meeting him with it in his hand, had said that
he was on the way to Darlingster, and would
save him a journey.

CHAPTER VII.

MEANWHILE, Margaret, with a lightened heart, had left the Hall, and was making her way to old Gilling's cottage. As she reached it, the old woman whom she was about to visit was seated in an armed-chair. Her deathlike, furrowed face was half turned from the window. Her brows were knit. Her eyes were fixed. And she was so much engrossed by deep thought that she did not hear when Margaret knocked, or when she gently opened the door. She was muttering indistinctly to herself, and when Margaret called, " Nurse, nurse," she started like one disturbed in sleep, and her mutterings became louder and clearer.

" Ay, ay," so they ran, " the promise went for nothink after we were married ; but you'll keep a promise to the dead, and it won't be long now,—it won't be long."

Margaret thought that she was wandering, and going close up to her, she put her hand upon her arm, and said,—

"Nurse, nurse, don't you know me? Won't you speak to me?"

Then a change passed over the face. A smile of sunshine chased away the shadows of gloom and anxiety by which it had been darkened, and for a moment the old woman looked as bright and loving as the young girl who was leaning over her.

"Lors, Miss Marget," she said, drawing the soft little hand caressingly into her own withered ones, "lors, Miss Marget, my darling, that ben't never you, come to see the old woman at last? I thought you was never coming no more."

"I have been wanting to come, every day, nurse, but——"

"Ah, I know," interrupted the old woman. "Miss Marget, you take your old nurse's advice. Don't you let that young fellow get his own way with you. He'll be coming it over you, if you don't mind what you're about, and then you won't find it easy to get

out of the puckle. He's a cunning one, is
Mr. Miles! Ay, I minds of him, that high,
a-stealing of the sugar-plums from little miss
when he thought no one wasn't looking. But
I was even with him, and I'll be even with
him again, for all he thinks himself so
safe!"

"What are you talking about, nurse? Mr.
Miles and I have nothing to do with each
other, now that we are too old to fight about
sugar-plums! What in the world can you
have got into your head about Mr. Miles
getting his own way with me?"

"Ah, there, Miss Marget, you knows well
enough what I means. I means as the
young gentleman what is gone off in such
hurry is worth a thousand of the other.
Don't you listen to any one who tells you
he ain't. You knows it well enough. I sees it
in the brightness of your eye, and the bloom
on your cheek."

The old woman was right. That peculiar
look for which no expression in words can
be found had come into Margaret's face,—
that look which follows upon the sudden

touch of an unseen messenger of life and love.

"Well, nurse," she laughed, "I certainly agree with you in liking Mr. Meredith the best of the two. He is very kind, is not he? You liked him, then?"

"Liked him, Miss Marget! Them must be bad 'uns or odd 'uns that would not like him. You know, Miss Marget, we can always tell when the eye looks true. There's some eyes what says, as they looks at you, that there's true gold in the words and in the smiles. There's other eyes that seems to be always saying that the words and the smiles and the gold itself be all cunning lies, sent by the devil to bring us to foolishness; and them's Mr. Miles' eyes. Let him keep his gold to himself, we don't want of it, to scorch our fingers off."

"Poor Mr. Miles! You are not fond of him, nurse," answered Margaret, rejoicing in the sense of sympathy with her pet aversion. "What has he done to you? Was it of him you were talking in your sleep, when you looked so cross, as I came in?"

"Talking?" cried the old woman, in a frightened tone. "Talking, was I? What was I talking, Miss Marget? I don't mind as I said anything! What did I say, then, Miss Marget?"

"You were asleep, nurse, so of course you don't remember all the foolish things you were saying about marriage, and promises, and death."

"Ay, ay, Miss Marget," returned nurse, while the old, fixed, troubled expression came back to the countenance. "Ay, ay, promises, marriage, death! Marriage, promises, death! It is all that, Miss Marget! It is all that! It won't be long, now, Miss Marget! It's the death that'll make it all right, dearie! Them that's cunning will find themselves disappointed, and them that's gone will come back again!"

"Dear nurse, you are dreaming again," said Margaret, tenderly. "There's plenty more of life for you on earth yet. We cannot spare you yet awhile."

"Ay, life, life," said the old woman musingly. "Miss Marget, do you see yon

chink in the door? I sometimes looks at it
till I sees it widen and widen, till it be big
enough for a little angel baby what I knowed
on earth to come through, and draw me after
him into the light, and into the fresh air, and
the burden drops off, and I can breathe,
like!"

The old woman stopped, panting. The
excitement which had given her strength for
a time, had, in the end, worn her out, and she
sank back fatigued, while her face became
rigid, and a more deathlike paleness passed
over it.

"You are tired, dear nurse, so I must
leave you. Good-bye; I shall come again
soon."

"Soon?—ay, it must be soon, Miss Marget! Promises, death, and marriage, my
dearie, that is what it will be," she said,
looking into the girl's loving eyes, which
were sorrowfully turned on the face of the
old nurse, for whom she had so tender an
affection. "Kiss me, kiss me, my lamb, for
memory of the days when you were your
nurse's sore heart's treasure and comfort."

So the darling face was pressed close against the lips of the dying woman, and after another lingering gaze, Margaret turned to leave the gardener's cottage.

As she walked home, after this interview with her old nurse, it seemed to her as if she had just awakened from a strange dream,—a dream which had left an impression that was not to be easily shaken off. The words of the old woman continually returned to her mind, giving her a strange and solemn feeling; and yet, at the same time, a sense of new life had come to her. As she thought of nurse's lost baby returning as an angel of life to rid her of the burden, whatever it might be, that was oppressing her heart, she remembered her own loss, her own burden! Charles Meredith's face seemed to come before her again, with the earnest inspired look in its eyes which had made him all at once appear to her so godlike. She pictured him no longer as sadly regretful, —the hope of his life having been destroyed by her word,—but she pictured him given up to an earnest work, and fancied that he was calling upon her to be earnest too. And she was resolved, with a sudden leap at her heart, that although at a distance, he should be as an angel of life to her, drawing her, as nurse had said, into a clearer, brighter, and purer atmosphere, where she might drop her burden of regret, and breathe and live. After all, he did not need her, his life might be blest without her, and in spirit they might be drawn near together, if only she might be unselfishly given up, as she felt sure he was given up, to the living of a true and earnest life.

"Who knows," she thought, "but that my unhappy mistake may be overruled for good, for I meant no harm, though it was hateful of me to be so blinded!" Besides, now that Sir John Grantham had written, all might speedily be well. "His letter must surely bring an answer, and,—who knows?—perhaps, perhaps, he may return! At all events I will be patient, and wait, and work! Surely the good that is working, unseen, must be stronger than the evil that is working; so there must be a good ending, there must be light to fall some time."

After this fashion she mused and resolved.

A thousand words, which had been dropped simply, with no pretension, and which had been carelessly heard by her, now came back to her mind, as so many proofs of a good and noble heart, and seemed to her, as she dwelt on them, replete with a power which might spur her on to be good and noble too.

"What would he say," she thought, "if he knew that I had not yet been to see that poor little consumptive boy, whom he pitied so much that day that we walked through the village, and saw the poor little tiny thin fellow sitting outside his cottage door, gasping for breath. Poor little Jack! I meant to have gone to see him the next day, but all those drives and picnics put him out of my head. It is an age since I went to the village; and what an immense amount of time I have wasted since the morning he went away! Poor nurse, I might as well have managed to get to her in the mornings. I will not neglect her again. What a fancy she seems to have taken to him."

CHAPTER VIII.

DURING her sleep that night many quaint and pretty fancies flitted through Margaret's brain. Nurse's face, bright and smiling, was mounted upon Jack's small body, as it flew towards her on angel wings, and drew her into a key-hole which led her into a church-yard covered with rose-trees, where she found herself standing by a grave, which seemed to be her own. Then she heard an anthem sung by a lovely voice, which she felt to be Charles Meredith's voice,—and the words, coming over and over again, and swelling out, and dying away, in such sweet music as she had never heard when awake, were always these, "Promises, marriage, death; promises, death, marriage." Charles Meredith's eyes, with the earnest look by which she was haunted day and night, were gazing upon her while the anthem sounded. But suddenly he vanished from her side, and the song was changed into marriage-bells, while Jane came up to her and said, "It's for old nurse, miss; they are to be married, she and Mr. Meredith." She awoke with a start at the seeming words. The church bell was tolling solemnly, and Jane was standing by her bedside.

"Jane," she said "what is the matter? What is the the bell tolling for? Why do you look so grave?"

"It is time for you to get up, miss," replied Jane, evading the question, while she retreated to the bedroom door. "I brought up your hot water half an hour ago."

"Can it be for poor little Jack?" thought Margaret, her heart sinking sadly, as she arose and went to her dressing-room. "And to think that I never went to see him again!"

On her way downstairs, when she was dressed, she met Jane, who said to her,—

"Miss Margaret, Gilling would be glad if you would go and see him as soon as you can."

"Where is he?"

"At home, miss. He has not been here to work yet. His wife was taken worse, miss, last night."

"Oh, Jane," cried Margaret, suddenly, it was for nurse that the bell was tolling!" And then came a rush of grief across her heart, and she burst into tears.

When she went to see the old man, she found him seated in the chair in which his wife had been sitting while she talked with her on the previous day. His hands were pressed tightly upon his knees. His head was bowed. And there was a look of grief on his face such as Margaret had never seen before. A young man was standing near him.

"Father, here's Miss Margaret come to see you," he said, as Margaret advanced silently to the chair, and stood by the old man's side.

"Eh? What, Miss Marget, be you here? Ah, you be too late—you be too late!"

And then he relapsed into silence, while the look of hard, bitter grief, which had for

a moment softened, crept back again over
his face.

" Jane told me that I might come to you,
Gilling," said Margaret, gently.

" To be sure, to be sure," returned the
old man ; " she was always terribly glad to
see you ! Ah, she won't see no one no
more !" And then, again absorbed by the
loneliness of his grief, he seemed to ignore
the presence of Margaret.

" I will go away, and come another time,"
said Margaret to the son ; " I only disturb
him now. I am glad he has you, Joe. When
did you come ? Were you in time ?

" Only just, miss. I didn't like the account
as I got from father, and missis give me
leave to come off at once, and I got here
last night. I found poor mother terrible
bad, to be sure.

" But she was conscious ? "

" Oh yes, miss, and asking for me, just
as I come in. ' Thank God,' she says, and
then I seemed in hopes that she was a bit
better for a while. But soon it all come
over her again, and she clutched hold of

father, and seemed beside herself, like, and
said, ' You promise, father,—you promise ? '
and then they looked at me, and father
whispered, and I come away; and when I
come back again I found mother's face
looking so bright, like, if you believe me,
miss, I thought I was in heaven, all of a
sudden. She just turned her eyes on me,
and then on father, and then——"

Here the poor fellow fairly broke down,
and sobbed like a child.

"God comfort you," said Margaret,
softly." You must think of that bright
look on her face, that you may feel as if
you were in heaven with her."

" Ay, and it's there still, miss ! Father
wants for you to see her. Will you please
to come up, now, miss? Father says as
no one hardly, but you, ben't good enough
to see her. You and parson, doctor and
Squire. Mr. Miles come, and was terrible
kind, and wanted to see her. But father
didn't half like it. He did not seem to
think as it was conformable, because, you
see, miss, mother hadn't used to be partial

to Mr. Miles. I can't seem to account for why she didn't use to like him, so terrible kind as he've always been. It seemed a'most as if she'd somehow got a cross in her mind about him. Ah, if she could only have known how kind he was when he come in this morning, giving father money for the funeral and all. It wasn't no use father saying as he would not have it, Mr. Miles wouldn't take no refusal."

" Mr. Miles has been to see you already, then ? "

" Yes, come almost immediate,—a'most before the bell began to toll; and father's been like this, a'most beside himself, seeming as if he see'd nothing and heard nothing on earth, ever since he was here. He looked scared like,—seemed as if the money scorched his fingers,—said as it wasn't respectful to the dead that he should have taken it. I a'most fancied once," here Joe lowered his voice mysteriously, " that he must have seen mother's ghost, he started so and looked so strange with his eyes; bless you, you might have thought he had stolen the money! And I'll warrant me there ben't a honester man in all the world!"

"I am sure there isn't," put in Margaret.

"Goes on a-muttering about his promise, —I know nothing about that; but I knows there ben't a faithfuller man than father to be found nowhere."

"I'm sure there is not," said Margaret, "and of course he cannot forget all your dear mother's fancies and wishes. She disliked Mr. Miles, you say, for some reason?"

"Yes miss; she didn't like none of them. Bless you, she hadn't a good word to say for my mistress, hadn't poor mother, for all she've been so kind to me,—a'most took me off father's hands when he married poor mother, the only mother I ever knowed anything about,—give me my schooling, you know, miss, and is a good mistress to me now, and says we shan't none of us never want for nothing, she and Mr. Miles. She be as good as her son. I can't say no more. But poor mother, she knew no better. She be in heaven, if ever any one was. As good a mother to me, she was, as if I'd been her own son twenty times over! Will you come up and see her, miss?"

"I think,—I think,—I think I had better not," began Margaret; but seeing a pained look pass over the young man's face, she reluctantly rose to follow him upstairs.

"Maybe you'll be able to rouse him, afterwards," he said, stopping to look anxiously round at the old man. "I can't rouse him nohow! He said as he wanted to see parson, had something to say to him, partic'ler; but when he come to him, bless you, he hadn't nothing to say to him, for all parson told him it was his duty not to rebel against the decree of the Almighty. Then he wanted to speak to doctor, but he hadn't nothing to say to him, neither; and for all he give him a mixture, he've gone on in the same way ever since. Then I tried what telling him about mistress would do, and how comfortable I was, and how many suits of clothes master give me; but, bless you, it only seemed to make him worse. He looked scared like, as though he'd seen the devil, and called out for mother to come and help him. Father, Miss Marget's going upstairs."

"Eh? what do you say, Joe?" said the old man, looking round. "Be Miss Marget going upstairs." God bless you, Miss Marget. She'd be pleased for you to come."

Margaret's heart beat as she approached the door, through which she was to be ushered, for the first time, into the mysterious presence of death! But as she drew near to the bed, and gazed at the beautiful marble face,—smooth and calm and smiling, with a smile such as that which the countenance of a sleeping child might have worn,—her sensations were very different from those which she had anticipated. Grief, anxiety, fear and hope, all seemed to have been suddenly hushed to rest. The recollection of her dream of the night before passed quickly through her mind, bringing with it a strange thrill, and all its scenes seemed to have been brought into sudden life. But it appeared as though even her memories had been transported into another world, and as if she had no longer anything to do with the outward things of this one. An angel voice from the land of her dream seemed to be saying, "He is not here! He is risen!" And then, as though in a rush of music through her heart, came the words, "I am the Resurrection and the Life." For a while she had stood silent, and now, as she looked up at Joe, it scarcely seemed to her as if it were her own voice in which she spoke the words,—

"She is not here! She is risen!"

To Joe it seemed indeed as if an angel had spoken; so bright, so almost heavenly, had the expression of her sweet face been, as she raised it to his while she gave the comforting message.

"Say that to father, miss," he said, as soon as his sobs would allow him to speak. "I seems in hopes as it might arouse him."

So together they went down to the old man.

"I have seen her, Gilling," she whispered. "How peaceful and beautiful it is! But it is not she! One feels that! One feels that she is more peaceful, more beautiful, in the life into which she has risen!"

The old man looked up, while a softer tone came over his face.

"Say it, miss, say them words," implored Joe.

"It was while we were looking on at it, you know, Joe, that we said, 'She is not here! She is risen!'" replied Margaret, in a hushed voice. And then tears came into her eyes. "Risen into life, not into distance," she added to herself; but the bereaved ones did not catch her thought, and before she could speak again,—

"No; she ben't here," returned the old man,—"she ben't here,—she ben't here, and I suppose one had ought to try to be thankful as she's up there. Do you think, miss, she cares to know, up there, what we does here? Do you think she'd be pleased, miss, if we do what she wants, and if we keeps our promises?"

"I am sure she would, Gilling; I think it would please her to see us trying to be good."

"And will it trouble her if we breaks our promises, and does things as ain't agreeable to her?"

"I don't know," said Margaret, quickly, looking puzzled; and then a new look, that was grave and bright at once, passing into her countenance, "HE is grieved when we do wrong," she murmured, musingly, half to herself, thus giving utterance to a fragment of the thought of her heart.

"Eh, Miss Marget? Would she care, up there? Would it trouble her?" put in the old man, impatiently.

"She must care more than ever," returned Margaret. "Perhaps untruth and wrong doing would bring a shadow so that she could not be made glad by seeing you!"

"And if things was all going contrary, and Joe was cast off, and we was to be hooted at, and to come to the work'us, would there come a shadow so that she could not see us Miss Marget?" asked Gilling.

Margaret began to think that the old man must indeed be beside himself.

"I hope nothing of the sort will happen," she replied. "If it should, perhaps God will send her to comfort you."

"Do you think so, Miss Marget?"

"At least, you feel sure that He will help you whatever comes?"

"Yes, miss, yes,—I knows that. I know as th' Almighty 'll help me. Yes,—I must do it! I must do it! I shouldn't mind if it wasn't for he," and he turned his eyes in the direction of his son, shaking his head and speaking softly, as though to himself.

Margaret's heart was full as she left the cottage door. She went to the village, thinking sadly, and pondering many things. But in spite of herself, glad and hopeful feelings leapt up through her heart, and seemed all the brighter for their contrast with her sad and heavy thoughts. After all, she was young, and life was full for her of delightful possibilities!

She called herself cold and heartless, but do what she would she could not stay the flow of natural spirits, which vexed her by its seeming incongruity. Her first visit in the village was to little Jack, whom she found leaning back luxuriously in an easy chair, with a ball and a top by his side and a coloured picture-book on his knee. He looked up eagerly as she approached, and then heaved a sigh, and blankly puckered up his face.

"I thought p'raps it was the kind gentleman come back," he said, as Margaret drew near.

"And you are disappointed?"

"Yes, ma'am.

"And who is the kind gentleman?" asked Margaret, her heart beating fast.

"The kind gentleman what give me these. He be gone away. When be he coming back?"

"Who is he? Don't you know his name? Is he the clergymen?"

"No."

"The doctor?"

"No. It be Mr. Meredy. He be gone, and he never come to say good-bye to me," said the child, plaintively.

" And was he very kind to you ? "

"He was terribly kind, and he promised to come and see me again."

" Did he often come to see you ? "

" A'most every day, and he telled me funny stories, and give me toys and books,— and I wants him ! "

And the poor little fellow closed his eyes and sighed wearily, while he pitifully puckered up his little wizened face.

"Perhaps he will come back again, dear," said Margaret, her eyes lighting up gladly as she spoke. " Perhaps I shall hear about him soon ! If I do, I will come and tell you the news."

The child's face brightened wonderfully.

"When do you think he will be here? Do you think he will come and see me directly he gets here, ma'am ? " he cried, eagerly.

" You must not be disappointed if he does not come soon, Jack," answered Margaret ; " but I will try to send a message to him from you, if you like. What shall it be ? "

" Dunnow ; but he must come *now !* "

said the boy, plantively. " I heard mother say as I was like to die soon, and I must see Mr. Meredy first. I doesn't want to die. They say as God will be kind to me in heaven ; but I don't think as He can be kinder nor Mr. Meredy, what give me this chair."

" But God made Mr. Meredy kind to you, dear," said Margaret.

" Did He? Then I love God, and I think as He'll send Mr. Meredy back to me !"

" I hope so, dear. Good-bye, I must go now. Shall I come again ? "

" Yes, soon, please ma'am. You be like him ! You have a kind look, just like him, on your face."

" Then I love God, and I think as He'll send Mr. Meredy back to me !" These words of little Jack's echoed again and again, like a lovely song, through Margaret's heart, while she walked about the village and home to her mother, and they made her feel un-reasonably hopeful,—hopeful and glad in the almost certain expectation that the post would speedily bring a letter from Mr.

Meredith to Sir John Grantham. But again and again, in the midst of her hopeful mood, she remembered, with a sorrowful sinking of her spirits, the grief of the village, and scolded herself for heartlessness.

As she was crossing the field in which old Gilling's cottage stood, she observed Joe Gilling standing outside the little wicket gate. He came near, and touching his hat, " I seems in hopes as father's a bit easier, miss," he said. " Mr. Miles come in again, and was terrible kind, to be sure. But when he went, father took on bad again,—seemed so strange I was a'most afraid he would have gone daft altogether; but by-and-by he seemed to get more quiet and natural-like. I heard him say as he'd let it 'bide till we had got the funeral over comfortable. ' She won't think as I am going to break my promise, because I puts off a bit,' he says. And then I falls to talking of how pleased mother'd be if she knew how decent the funeral was to be, and that Mr, Miles was going to give him a fine new black coat and all ; and so I got him to cheer up a bit."

Margaret wondered to herself, as she continued her journey homewards.

"What can this secret be that seems to be troubling old Gilling's conscience?" she thought. "And what makes Miles so marvellously charitable all of a sudden? He is certain to be up to some mischief whenever he pretends to be particularly good! It always was so when we were children."

CHAPTER IX.

MARGARET'S first thought on waking the next morning was, " Perhaps there may be a letter from Mr. Meredith; " her second brought the sorrowful recollection that the old nurse who had been as a mother to her in her childhood was dead !

Her first visit was to the Hall, after which, —her heart sick with disappointment, for there was no letter,—she wandered towards old Gilling's cottage, to sympathise with the mourners there, and then on to the village to be soothed by poor little Jack's loving praise of her friend.

On the following day, again the stillness of her thoughts of death was disturbed,— first by hope and then by disappointment. For again there was no letter.

Then came the day of the funeral; and

she told herself that no earthly hopes and fears, no fond regret or vain longing, must be permitted to break in upon its solemn calm. When the presence of death seemed to be shadowing all the earth, it would surely be sacrilege to dream of earthly bliss! When glimpses of an unseen life " behind the veil " opened, as it seemed, from time to time upon her vision, could it be right to care for the life or death of hopes connected with earth? When others were in sore grief, was it not mean and selfish to let her mind dwell on anxieties or hopes of her own?

Thus musing, she strolled slowly through the wood, and across the boundary line dividing the grounds of the cottage from those of Grantham Hall. But on catching sight of Sir John Grantham, her quiet musings suddenly ceased, and while her heart gave a great bound, she hurried forward to meet him, and in a moment was raising to his, unconsciously wistful and inquiring eyes. Something tenderly pitiful in his face seemed to stay on her lips the question that she had meant to ask.

"Childie," he said, after a minute's pause, while he caressingly stroked her face with his big hand,—"childie, I begin to think it would be as well for you and me to try to forget all about that gay young man who made believe to be so fond of us t'other day. He don't seem to be in a hurry to write to us, or to care much to get our letters, and, from all I can learn, he appears to be enjoying his absence from us fully as much as he enjoyed our company."

"Perhaps," answered Margaret, as quietly as she could, "perhaps your letter has not reached him."

"So I said to Lady Grantham this morning; but it came out that the young gentleman had written to Miles since his receipt of my letter, and had sent a message which Miles had forgotten to deliver,—a cool sort of message enough,—to the effect that he was much obliged for my letter, and hoped to write when he had more leisure. And how do you suppose his busy days to be occupied? In no less arduous a manner than dancing, and picnic·ing, and love-making, and all the rest of it! Perhaps Miles will indulge you with a reading of the lively account if you ask him."

"Miles!" contemptuously cried Margaret, with a reproachful glance into Sir John Grantham's face,—"Miles!" And then, making some hasty excuse, she turned away from him, and flew, with passsionate footsteps, to hide herself in the deepest shade of her favourite wood.

With a grave smile, Sir John Grantham gazed after her until she was out of sight. "Miles!" he said aloud, to himself, mimicking her scornful tone of voice. "Ay, Miles! Miss Margaret. But you are like all the women," so his thoughts continued to run, "doubting where it pleases your prejudice to doubt, and believing where your fancy bids you believe! Women, did I say? Pshaw! I have been as big a fool myself as the silliest of them all! That stranger lad took my fancy, and I chose all at once to transform him into a fancied paragon of perfection, and exalt him into the image in which I would have chosen to see my own son formed,

had he lived to grow up ; while for my poor
nephew,—because his tastes do not happen
to chime in with those of his boorish old
uncle,—because he offends my taste,—because, forsooth, his features take their pattern
rather from those of madam than from those
of my poor brother,—-because,—nay,

> " The reason why I cannot tell,
> I do not like thee, Dr. Fell ! "

This is the long and short of it, I believe.
But we must learn to conquer our prejudices,
you and I, Miss Margaret; we must learn to
see merit where we are assured that merit
lies ; and who knows but that on some happy
wedding-day, when our eyes have been fully
opened, we may look back laughingly on all
our follies, and be ' happy ever after ? ' Poor
child, poor child,'' concluded the baronet, in
an audible murmur,—" poor child ! Well, it
is the way of the world.   Heigho ! we have
all had our dreams and our disappointments,
in our time, and the grief passes away like the
joy, and we almost forget that it has ever
been ! Forget, do we ? Forget? Nay ! not

on this side the grave, whatever we may do on the other ! ''

Margaret, meanwhile, was sobbing her heart out in her hidden corner. It was not that she for an instant believed in her lover's fickleness. Had this been her belief, not a sob, not a tear, would have been allowed to escape her. But her trust in Charles Meredith was not to be so easily shaken. Even before the memorable evening on which her heart, as it were, had been allowed to feel the touch of his, and had been inspired with the knowledge that she loved him, her woman's instinct had told her that he was true to the core. And now, she could almost sooner have doubted the evidence of her own senses than have lost faith in the reality of his love. She was not even troubled by the thoughts that the coming years would bring changes, that she had no right to expect him to be constant to her, when she had told him that she did not love him, that it would be only natural for him to teach himself to forget her, and to learn to love another. She did not think of change. She did not look into the

future. She only felt that the present was
utterly dark and dreary : and the hopes that
she had been cherishing had been swept
away so suddenly by the baronet's hasty words,
that, in her youthful inexperience, it seemed
to her that she could never, never, rise again
into happiness. She realised, all in a moment,
that he whom she loved best in all the world
was far away out of her reach, that all her
chances of hearing about him were over,
that all possibility of letting him know that
she returned his love was at an end ! Miles
might be telling a thousand untruths about
her, which she would never find any means
of refuting, and Charles Meredith, unsuspici-
ous of deceit, believing the false representa-
tions, might be thinking of her as a heartless
flirt ; but no, she could not dream of him as
harbouring a bitter thought of her, she
could only picture him with the look of deep
sorrow in his face which had so often haunted
her sleeping and waking dreams, since the
night on which she had seen him last. She
could only picture him in sore, sore grief,
lonely, and far out of the reach of her sym-

pathy. Oh, to be by his side but for one moment! Oh, to be able to comfort him, even
for an instant! In the agony of her longing
and her dreariness, she cried aloud, "Oh
God! oh God! I cannot, cannot bear it!"
The summer breeze and the buzzing insects
seemed to be repeating her cry, and she
failed to hear the still small Voice, which was
surely murmuring in the depths of her spirit
the words, "I will be with you!" Her
passionate heart was so full of its woes that
she did not remember that a loving Messenger was by her side, ready to carry to him
she loved the sympathy she longed to give.
So her tears and sighs obtained for her no
relief.

Suddenly the church bell began to toll!

Margaret had forgotten all about poor
old nurse, the village sorrow, and the
coming funeral! And now, as she roused
herself, and set out, mechanically, on her
walk to the church, it seemed to her, in
her egoism, that the sorrow even of the
chief mourners on the occasion was easy,
was almost nothing, in comparison with

the one by which her own heavy heart was absorbed. The old woman had long been failing, and now was at peace! Her husband would soon join her. Her stepson had the world before him, and would find a thousand new interests, a thousand joys, to beguile him from his grief! "At least," she thought, "their grief is a gentle one and full of consolation; they know where she is, and look forward to seeing her again!"

Yet soon she found herself tenderly and regretfully remembering the old nurse, looking, in fancy, once more upon the kind old face, and hearing again the strangely-spoken farewell words; and, as in her dream of a few nights back, the bell seemed to be slowly tolling out the poor old woman's deathsong, "Promises, marriage, death; promises, death, marriage." She ceased to think! The words in her memory, rising and falling with the solemn music to which she had unconsciously set them, appeared to be lulling her mind into a sort of death-like stupor.

But suddenly the glorious verse, " I am the Resurrection and the Life ! " uttered in the vicar's clear, sonorous tones, struck upon her ear, and brought to her heart a momentary touch of life and light.

" The Resurrection and the Life ! " Yes, not only was there an unseen life for the dead old woman, but there was One, The Life Himself, in Whom dead hopes, a lost love, absent friends, all might live, all might be found again !

Then the shadow of death came over her once more, and, wearied out by the intensity of her feeling, she passed in dull apathy through the wonderful Burial Service, looking with almost absent pity upon the bowed figure of the sorrowing husband, accusing herself, secretly, of heartlessness, and dream. ing, in spite of this self-accusation, that if Charles Meredith were standing and kneeling by her, a sorrowful season would be transformed, for her, into a season of transcendent joy.

The service over, she sauntered slowly homewards by the fields. When she got to the meadow in which Gilling's house stood, she caught sight of some one just going in at the cottage door, and in another moment Joe came out at the little garden gate.

" Thank you, miss," he said, as Margaret drew near. " Father was terribly pleased to see you at the funeral,—showed such respect and all; and did any one good to hear the neighbours say as you looked so haggard, and seemed to be taking on so, a'most as if it had been your own mother. I'm a-going after parson for father. He seems to be took with a desire to see parson again; still got something partic'ler on his mind as he wants to be rid of. It 'll be best for him to have out with it; but I didn't like to leave him alone, so as Mr. Miles was coming by, he said as he'd stay with him a bit."

" A nice person, Miles, to have to comfort you in grief! " said Margaret to herself, with a grim smile, as Joe walked on. And in spite of her private trouble, she found herself wondering, with some degree of

interest, what old Gilling's secret burden
could be, and thinking, with a kind of
fear of she knew not what, about Miles
Grantham's pretended kindness to him.

"What can he want with the poor old
man?" she wondered. "He is certain to
be up to some sort of mischief, wherever
he is, or whatever about."

Instinctively, she turned in at the little
wicket gate. Miles was speaking in loud
tones to suit the old gardener's deafness,
and Margaret caught the words,—

"He is a fine youth. It would be a pity
to spoil his prospects," and then followed
a feeble murmur from the old man, followed
by Miles' answer,

"Ah, but she would be wiser now. She
loved your son as well as you do, Gilling,
and she would not wish you to break an
old promise for a new one,—and all for
no good! Where is the use of taking up
old troubles that have been forgotten long
ago? There, this will keep you in decent
black for a long time to come."

"No, no, Mr. Miles; she had always used

to tell me as I was too fond of dross,"
feebly remonstrated the old man.

The conversation was only partially heard
by Margaret, but as she glanced inadvertently
through the open window, she saw the old
gardener's eyes turned, half sadly, half
eagerly, on a little heap of gold that lay
on the table before him. Her knock was
answered by Miles, who, as she entered,
said, in a tone of affected jocularity,—

"Here is Gilling quarrelling with his
bread and butter, Margaret, you must come
and say what you can, to try to keep up his
heart. Gilling, here is Miss Margaret, so
I'll leave you now."

"Eh? What, Miss Marget, be that
you?" said Gilling, looking up with a
softened face, and pushing away the money.
"Ah, she was always glad to see you! So
you've come to see the old man, and have a
talk about her what's gone? There, take
your money, Master Miles, and be off with
you."

"Good-bye, Gilling, but I shall be hurt
if you don't keep the money. I am going

away, soon, you know, and perhaps I shall
not see you any more."

And then he went, while Gilling, with
a sigh, half of trouble, half of relief,—
almost satisfaction,—glanced at the gold on
the table before him.

In a few minutes Joe came back.

"Parson 'll be here directly, father," he
said.

The old man shuffled uneasily on his
chair.

"Don't know that I want anything of
parson," he said, rather peevishly. "What
do you go off in such a hurry to call parson
for? Any one's best left alone when he's
in trouble. No one can't do him no good.
There's Mr. Miles been here, a-bothering of
me. I'm sure I don't want his gold. Put
it away, somewhere, Joe, will yer? Miss
Marget, I forgot yer," he added, as Margaret rose to take her leave. "I'm not
rightly myself to-day."

"Something odd, something that I can't
make out!" thought Margaret. "But what
does it matter to me?" Presently she

came across Mr. Bowles, the vicar, walking with Miles Grantham. He was a big, broad man, with a genial, easy-going expression of countenance. They were walking together very energetically, and did not see Margaret. The clergyman was apparently much impressed by some remark of Miles'.

"He is a queer old fellow, I know," he was saying, as Margaret passed within earshot. "I have never been able to make head or tail of him. I should not wonder if you are right in what you say."

"He is harmless, poor old buffer," at present, returned Miles; "but I am convinced there is a screw loose somewhere. I shall be curious to know what he says to you. He talks as if he was oppressed by some secret crime, and his son is convinced that it is all a delusion. His wife seems to have been down upon him about his love of money, and this weighs so much upon his mind that I could hardly get him to accept a trifle from me just now. I feel to owe him something for——"

"What business has Miles to interfere

about old Gilling ? Why cannot he let him alone ? I suppose he wants to gain a character for benevolence with the vicar," thought Margaret, charitably, as she moved aside, out of hearing, and then her thoughts returned to her own heart's trouble.

The next day old Gilling took to his work again. He talked to Margaret, as usual, about his garden concerns, carried about with him his wonted expression of countenance, and appeared to have buried in some secret corner of his being both his grief and the burden that had seemed to be troubling his conscience.

" Parson cheered him up a bit," said Joe, in answer to Margaret's inquiry. " He has a cheerful way with him, and he told father as he'd best let things 'bide as they were, and not be bothering hisself. So he's seemed more natural, like, since, as if he'd sort of put a cloud away from him. I heerd him a-muttering as parson must know best, and likely mother'd know better than she did now, and would see as things as has been done couldn't be undone all in a

minute, partic'ler where there's other people
to think of besides oneself. I don't know
what it's all about, Miss Margaret, and I
ain't going to trouble myself to find out.
It ain't no business of mine, so that I sees
father sort of like his natural self again, and
taking heart a bit, before I leaves him."

Neither, Margaret thought, was it any
business of hers; and she soon let the
matter pass away from her remembrance.

CHAPTER X.

LIFE in Darlingster and its neighbourhood
now went quietly on, without much outward
stir or change. Joe's leave of absence from
service came to an end. Gilling gradually
subsided into his old accustomed placid
self,—an indefatigable, energetic gardener,
who might have been supposed never to
have known grief or anxiety, excepting such
as bore reference to the shrubs and plants
amidst which he moved and worked.—Miles
Grantham left the Hall. Alice Craycroft's
almond-shaped eyes grew more pensive.
Summer days gradually waned away into
autumn ones. Picnics and lawn dances
ceased. The postman still paced daily
backwards and forwards between Darlingster and Grantham, but brought no letter
that materially affected the current of ex-

istence at the Hall or at The Cottage. Mrs.
Willoughby continued to be troubled by
headache, to be regularly more or less
languid, and nervously irritable, in the
mornings, to be irregularly excited into
energy by some whim or fancy, towards
the end of the day. And Margaret was
guietly learning to adapt herself to the
alteration which a few summer weeks had
wrought in her own individual inner life.
Little difference was marked in her by
others. She read, worked, drew, played,
attended tenderly upon her mother, visited
the poor, laughed and talked, and rambled
about the woods, just as she had done
before. Perhaps she now preferred those
employments which occupied her hands,
and left her thoughts free. Perhaps she
oftener now appeared to be in a hurry to
shut up her book and wander restlessly out
of doors. Perhaps Lady Grantham would
oftener have occasion to remark, disapprov-
ingly,—

"My darling, you look fagged; you tire
yourself to death with those everlasting

poor people. I must really send for Miles, to beguile you on to 'Hero's' back!"

Or Sir John Grantham would vex her by looking at her anxiously, and then saying, lightly,—

"She is getting '.pale and interesting,' this girl! Mrs. Willoughby; you will have to send her away into the gay world, to bring back some roses."

Or, worst of all, Mrs. Willoughby herself would distress her, by exclaiming peevishly,—

" My dear Margaret, it is all very well to be benevolent; but you appear to me to have taken up your abode in the village for good and all, and to have forgotten that home duties come first! I wanted some lavender drops this morning, but there was no one to fetch them for me, and my head was so bad that I could not get up from the sofa to ring the bell for Jane." Or, "I am not complaining, my dear, but I should like to have you a little more with me!" Or it might be, " My love, you are looking very sentimental; I wish I could see you improving your mind a little more. You

seem quite to have given up working at your
history or German ! "

But, on the whole, they let the girl go
pretty much her own way, and saw little
reason to disturb themselves about her at
present. There were times when her high
animal spirits got the better of all else, and
her natural merriment was free and unre-
strained. And at those other times, when
her heart was weary of present things, and
was dejected through regretful wanderings
into the happy past, there was no one to see
the pathetic expression of hopeless longing
that would steal over her face, while her eyes
seemed to be gazing far, far away into the
indefinite, as though in search of something
which they might never find. But there
were better, truer times than these. There
were moments when the indefinite was
changed into the infinite, where the eyes of
her imagination seemed to find a bright and
peaceful resting-place. There she saw
visions of that which was and was to be,
and heard angel-whisperings, which assured
her that 'love which knows no earthly

close' may obtain in a pure and immortal world full and unceasing satisfaction.

From the heights of her pure dreamland, she sometimes came down to common life, with her countenance transfigured into a strange beauty, which, if Sir John Grantham chanced to come across her, caused him to glance at her with uneasy admiration. "She looks as if she were ready for her wings," he would say to himself, and were about to fly away up there, where the other bright ones are gone to, out of my dull sight!"

Margaret's inner life, however, was not all made up of sad musings and bright imaginings. Sorrow such as hers stirs up the mind to its depths, and sets to work a thousand dark and difficult questions. Who was to answer these questions for the lonely girl? Who was to bring back to her her former careless and contented trust in things which had been to her as a distant prospect, adding, by its vague and shadowy beauty, to the pleasure of her bright and happy life? There was no one to whom she could speak,—no one who could answer

these 'infant cryings in the dark!'—no
one but the One who finally replied to
Job : the One who at once justified and re-
proved him for his complaints, who touched
him with the reality for which he had craved,
and made him understand the secret work-
ings of His just and loving might, amidst the
seeming success of injustice, pain, and evil.
Perhaps he would also bring relief to this
poor desolate child. Perhaps He, Who, in
spite of His love and power, had suffered
her to feel the bitter pain of human loss and
absence, and had permitted it to arouse that
bitterest agony, the dread lest Divine love had
no existence in reality,—perhaps He would
Himself bring the blessed remedy. Perhaps
in His answer, and in the touch of his loving
hand, she would learn that, amidst all uncer-
tainties, He, at least, was sure,—He at least
understood the peculiarities of her trouble,
—that He was her Guide, and the Guide of
her absent friend,—that, amidst the dark and
evil deeds that others were working in the
world, He was working good,—that, amidst
her own mistakes and follies, He was work-

ing wisdom. Perhaps when things seemed darkest for herself and others, she would still hear his voice telling her that 'good' would be the 'final goal of ill.'

As has been said, her great relief, when oppressed by restless longings, was in active work. The mere movement, the having something to do that had no reference to her trouble, and that yet did not force her thoughts away from it, soothed her in spite of herself. Then while she was passing from cottage to cottage, certain familiar words suddenly darted into her mind, with a new and sweet meaning. 'Be ye steadfast, unmovable, always abounding in the work of the Lord, forasmuch as ye know that your work is not in vain in the Lord.' This last verse of the lesson in the Burial Service had caught her wandering attention on the day of old nurse's funeral, and had seemed to her to give but cold and dreary comfort. "Work, lonely work! How was it to be borne! What good was there in it?" So had she, wearily, rather felt than thought! For all life at the moment had appeared

to her sinking heart to be nothing better
than a useless blank. But now, with the
remembrance of the words, there seemed
to come to her a mysterious touch, as it were,
from afar, to tell her that her work was not
in vain,—to tell her that it was done in unison
with one at a distance, and was linking her
life with his in the unseen eternal world. In
fancy she saw again the steadfast, earnest
look that had thrilled through her, as though
it had been the gaze of a prophet who was
rapt into the Invisible, and was hearing the
message that called him to fulfil a noble
mission.

Again she seemed to perceive, as though
for the first time, that this seer was godlike ;
and, as though inspired by him with redoubled
strength, she went about her work with fresh
life and energy. Must she be accused of
idolatry and earthly motive ? If it were so,
at least her thought was pure and unworldly,
and was leading the way to a higher and
holier sense of spiritual union with One unseen. And gradually she lost herself in the
interests and concerns of others. The sym-

pathy which had been somewhat forced and absent, grew to be hearty and genuine.

Her chief interest was poor little Jack; but it was an interest which was slowly fading away from her, with the poor little boy's feeble life. Day by day he grew thinner, the lines about his face became sharper, his eyes grew larger and brighter, his breathing became weaker and more painful. But the winter went by, and left him still alive ; the bleak winds of March, the April showers, and the May blossoms came and went, and left him lingering still. And it was not until the hot days of August drew round again that the messenger called him, and he passed away.

Poor little Jack ! Unconsciously, he had done a work in his short life. He had soothed, softened, and strengthened one in great distress. He had been to her as an angel from the far-away world of her love. He had given her tangible proof, if proof were needed, that he whom she loved best in the world had a good, and gentle, and noble heart. It was a proof which she could bring forward, she liked to think, if others chose to dispute the fact. Therefore, although little Jack may have been an unimportant mover in the scenes of Margaret Willoughby's life, it would be ungrateful and unfair to leave him altogether out of its story. Each day throughout the autumn on which Margaret had gone to visit the sick boy, he had asked,—

"Have you heard from Mr. Meredy? Is he coming?"

And long after Margaret had ceased expecting to hear or see anything of her friend, the child had continued to ask the same question.

"Not yet, Jack," she had answered,— "not yet; we must be patient. God will let him come to us in good time."

But as the boy's end had seemed to be drawing nearer, Margaret's reply had become different.

"Perhaps, Jack," she had answered, often with a choking voice—"perhaps you will find him where you are going."

And then Jack's face had brightened, and

he had talked eagerly of all that he would
do in the fair home to which he was going,
—how he would teach the " angel-children "
to love Mr. Meredy as he did, and would
sing songs with them about the kind things
that the good gentleman had done for him
when he was on earth.   For Margaret had
told the boy many an " angel story," and
had tried to make the mysterious land to
which he was hastening seem to him real,
and bright, and loving, that he might not
fear to find himself a stranger there.   But
tremblingly and sadly had she listened to
his gentle talk.   Oh, that she, too, might go!
—that she, too, might pass away into that
pure and loving home,—that she might find
him there, at rest !   So had she sometimes
wearily sighed.   At last, one day,—it was a
day in August, a burning day, with scarcely
a breath of air, the gardens brilliant with
flowers, the corn-fields rich with their golden
harvest, the world looking beautiful and
happy,—Margaret was on her way to the
death-bed of little Jack.   A thousand
thoughts were busy in her mind.   A thou-

sand feelings were making her heart beat
quickly, and were half dimming her eyes.
A thousand voices seemed to be whispering
to her, through the still atmosphere, of by-
gone days, and scenes of the past rose up
vividly before her eyes. It was the anniver-
sary of the day on which she had last seen
Charles Meredith! Should she ever see
him again on earth? She seemed to be
with him in spirit, as she entered Jack's sick
room. She found the dying child changed
indeed,—but with his face not one whit the
less bright than it had been in his stronger
days; it even almost seemed to her, as she
looked at it, to be shining with a strange
unearthly light.

"Miss Marget," he said, none the less
eagerly for the painful gasps which interrupted his speech—"Miss Marget, I've
been a-thinking,—seems to me as I'm a'most
sure to find Mr. Meredy there, for you says
as it's because Jesus loves me, as He's
coming to fetch me, and I don't think as He
could have done without Mr. Meredy all this
time! It's been bad enough for me, but it

won't matter soon. Don't you think as He must have got him there by this time?"

The question was asked wistfully, and with a momentary touch of painful doubt. And Margaret checked her fast-rising tears, and smiled a smile which might have been caught from the world to which Jack was hastening, and tenderly touched the little thin cold hand and whispered soothingly, "He will make it all right for you, dear."

Then Jack looked quite happy again.

"I'll tell Him about you, Miss Marget," he said; "I'll tell Him as you talked about Him, and how good you was, and as you'll come soon. I'll tell them both about you." And for the moment Margaret was able to enter fully into his gladness, and it almost seemed to her that she was being drawn with him into a heaven such as children ween of, 'behind the veil, behind the veil.'

As he finished speaking, he sank back, and weariedly closed his eyes, and with a happy smile upon his face he fell into a half-conscious doze. From time to time he

murmured, now the name of Mr. Meredith,
then a holier name, and it seemed as if the
two were confused together in his mind.
Margaret remained in the still room for a
few minutes, and then took her leave, while
the little boy's mother and sister sat by the
bedside, to watch for the end. And so
Margaret had looked her last on the little
angel-face, and had lost what had seemed
to her the only outward thing that had
formed for her, as it were, a link with him
who was far away. Musing sadly, she
turned from the village into the churchyard,
and seated herself beneath the old yew tree.
From her quiet corner, where she was herself
safe from observation, she saw villager after
villager trudge by,—for the churchyard was
a thoroughfare,—and presently old Gilling
entered from the field in which his cottage stood.
As he passed on his way to his wife's grave,
he seemed lost in thought, while thrusting
his hand into his pocket, as though to
make sure that some treasure there was
safe,—

"Ah," he said to himself, "she didn't like

him--she didn't like him; as for that, like is
like, and gold is *gold*. It ben't them as is liked
as does you the most good; and Mr. Miles is
good to Joe, and we'll a'most make a gentle
man of the lad maybe, in time. I han't forgot
my promise to the old woman, neither, but the
time for keeping of it ben't come yet; and
she'll be wiser where she be's now: knows
as it ain't no use making a to-do, to do no
good to nobody. 'Tain't for myself—'tain't
for myself. I don't want to do nothing with
it for myself; but it is comfortable, like, to
know that it is all safe for the lad. Any one
likes to feel as he's got a bit of his own, if
he didn't a-bring it into the world with him,
and can't a-take of it away with him. Well,
my time 'll come, I suppose, like the rest;
but I'm hale and hearty yet, and seems in
hopes as I've got a good many years afore
me, and a deal of flowers to look after, afore
I has to be put in the coffin. I wish I could
bring the old woman back again, though!
Ah, times is changed, times is changed,
since we come along and went through that
there door for to be married! We was very

comfortable, for all she worrited me about the money and that.''

Here again thrusting his hands into his pockets, old Gilling retraced his steps across the field to his cottage.

CHAPTER XI.

IT was time for Margaret, also, to return home, but she waited, watching, until the old man's slow footsteps had borne him out of her sight. She watched him, with curious wondering thoughts. She had only been an involuntary hearer of a word or two, here and there, where he had muttered his thoughts audibly; but the pre-occupied expression of his face, and his attitude as he bent over his wife's grave, had brought back to her his strange behaviour at the time of the old woman's death, and her own passing wonder and curiosity. But she was soon engrossed again by her sorrowful and yet peaceful musings, and as she took her way home by the fields, she was careful to keep her distance from the gardener's house, being in no mood for conversation with him. She was not to escape, however, so easily.

"Miss Marget," called the old man, from his garden gate—"Miss Marget, be that you? I've a bit o' news for yer."

"Have you, Gilling?" replied Margaret, drawing nearer, and speaking with assumed interest. "I am afraid, though, that I must not stop to hear it, for I am rather in a hurry."

"Be you on your way home? You'll find company there. There's been an arrival, Miss Marget," said the old man, with a cunning wink and a pleased smile, intended to enhance the excitement of suspense in his hearer's mind.

Suddenly a wild hope, an expectation,— which, seen through her imagination, appeared almost like certainty,—rushed into her heart, and agitated her almost beyond control.

"We do not expect any one. Who can have come? One of my uncles?" she managed to say.

"Better nor that," returned the old man, slowly shaking his head. "Can't you guess, Miss Marget? Well, then, I must tell you,

I suppose. Who should it be but Mr. Miles, to be sure?—come down to the Hall, but didn't stay a minute there,—was down at The Cottage all in such a hurry and fuss as never was,—stays for a word with me, though, but I sees as he's a-dying to get to the house, and says I to myself, 'I know who he's a-come after!' He left me in a pretty hurry, and I hear tell as he asked to see missis very partic'ler. You'll find him there now, if you be quick."

"Quick?" Poor Margaret! Would it be possible for her ever to be quick again? The sudden revulsion of feeling had seemed in a moment to take all life and spirit out of her. A sense of faintness came over her, and she would have fainted away if strong desire had not given her strength to resist.

"What's the matter, Miss Marget?" said the old man, his tone changed to one of alarm. "You was all in a flush a moment ago, and now you looks like to die!"

"I am tired, Gilling," answered Margaret, forcing a smile. "Give me a glass of water, please, and then I must make haste home."

" There, there, sit ye down, and rest a bit, Miss Marget, for you don't look fit to walk home."

But Margaret was soon on her legs again, and strong for the walk, trying to laugh at herself for her folly, and grumbling, mentally, at the annoying news she had received; which, after all, however, she thought, did not much signify. Things were simply as they had been, neither better nor worse, only she had made a fool of herself for a moment. At the garden entrance she met Jane, who exclaimed, as she held the gate open,—

" Why, Miss Margaret, what is the matter? You look as if you'd seen a ghost, or was one yourself. Your mamma sent me to look for you. She thought as you was never coming, and was afraid as you might have fallen in with tramps, or something. She wished me to tell you to go to her directly you come."

" Has she been wanting me?" asked

Margaret. I'm not so very late, am I ? "

" You forget, miss, how nervous your mamma is," answered Jane, reproachfully.

" I never knew her to get nervous because I did not come in till seven o'clock before !" thought Margaret. And she went into the drawing-room, quite prepared to find her mother in a very unusual state of mind.

" My dear Margaret, what have you been about all this time ? " was Mrs. Willoughby's greeting. I was beginning to get quite anxious.

" I am very sorry mamma, but—why ? Am I very late ? What is it ? Have you been wanting me ? Has anything happened ? Is anything the matter ? " asked Margaret.

" Sit down, my dear child," replied her mother, in an evident fluster of nervous excitement. " I have a great deal to say to you. Some one has been here,—I shall leave you to guess who,—some one who loves you very dearly. He has been talking about you, but I shall not tell you what he said. He must plead his own cause with you to-morrow ; he has my free permission. Oh, Margaret, what a noble heart you have won ! You surely will not trifle with it any longer ! "

" What do you mean, mother ? " cried Margaret flushing up and speaking rather indignantly. " Has Miles dared,—after all that I said to him last year,—after———"

" He told me of his conversation with you last year, my dear," interrupted her mother. " He owns that he was too precipitate. He owns that his strong feeling led him to be unjust to you."

"'Unjust'! Oh, mother, if you could have known the way he spoke,—if you could have seen and heard all, you would never wish me to speak to him again ! "

" My dear child, this is folly. You must make allowance for lovers' feelings. Everything is fair in love and war, you know," returned her mother, with a little irritating laugh, which almost drove Margaret out of her mind.

" Mamma, please don't talk in that way,

she said, pleadingly; "I cannot bear it. It has been so sad this afternoon, because of poor little Jack,—and I am so tired! May we please talk no more about Miles to-night?"

You are very ungrateful," returned her mother, querulously, "*very* ungrateful! You little know," she continued, with a somewhat tragic air—"you little know what he has borne for your sake during the past year!—how he has striven with himself,—how, during his flying visits to the Hall, he has refrained from utter ing a word of love to you!—how, at the risk of breaking his heart, he has let his devotion flow silently on, all that he might keep his promise to you! He hoped that you would appreciate this conduct, that, at at least, he might have won something of your regard; he hoped he read approval in your countenance! But it seems he is to be disappointed, that all his pain and self-denial are to go for nothing!"

"All this is humbug!" cried Margaret, half under her breath. "It is hardly a

year!" she went on, aloud, "since he gave
his promise,—I don't consider that he has
kept it properly. And if he had a grain of
wisdom in his composition, he would know
that there was no chance of my ever learning
to like him."

"Then you mean to break his heart! You
mean to break all our hearts! You don't
care what you make your mother suffer, so
that you may get your own way. Oh,
Margaret! Margaret! have you no sympathy, no heart, no——"

Here Mrs. Willoughby leaned back in
her easy chair, and subsided into hysterical
sobbing. In a moment Margaret was by
her side.

"Mother, dear mother,—mother, darling,
don't, please don't! I can't bear to vex you.
I would do anything to please you,—you
know I would. But—but you don't understand. Let us talk about this another time!"

The *eau-de-cologne* and camphor julep
and salts were brought into requisition, and
by degrees Mrs. Willoughby was restored to
something like composure.

" Well, my dear," she said, more cheerfully and more kindly, " I dare say you will see things very differently to-morrow, when you have had a good night's rest. I don't wonder at your having been a little taken by surprise. Run away now, darling, and get ready for tea, and then you shall tell me about all you have been doing."

" And you are better, mother dear? I have not made your head really worse?" said Margaret, tenderly.

But she knew that her mother would suffer the next morning for the evening's excitement and agitation of which she had been the unwilling cause, and weary, heavy-hearted, remorseful, and indignant, she went her way in obedience to her mother's behests.

" How is it to end?" she asked herself, hopelessly. " Shall I kill mamma if I refuse to have anything to say to that odious humbug? Something, surely, must turn up to make things right! "

CHAPTER XII.

THE night had passed. The hour at which Mrs. Willoughby had hoped that her daughter would "see things differently" had arrived. Miles Grantham had paid an early visit to The Cottage, and had done Margaret the honour to ask her to be his wife. The honour had not been accepted. And the heir of Grantham Hall was standing outside the door of The Cottage, a disappointed, sore, and indignant man. All his precautions, all his prudence, all his good behaviour, had been thrown away. He had gone into Margaret's presence armed with her mother's favour. He had put on a modest demeanour. He had avoided all those looks and tones which he knew to be hateful to her, and had been in his manner at once straightforward, earnest, and gentle. And yet,—she had refused him point-blank! He lingered for a moment with his hand on the door, as though half in doubt as to whether the battle were indeed yet lost, and then, with a gesture of contempt, he turned away, hurried along the Darlingster road, and presently stopped short on the threshold of a large and handsome house, where he knew that he should find consolation of a kind very dear to his vain spirit.

Margaret, meanwhile, sat gravely thoughtful in the drawing-room of The Cottage. She felt not the least touch of pity for her rejected suitor; not the faintest shadow of tender or friendly regret that it was not in her power to grant him the boon that he had asked of her; not the smallest particle of gratitude or gratification on account of the honour that had been done to her. Her answer had been polite, prompt, and decided. But now that Miles was no longer present, her thoughts reverted anxiously to her mother,—her poor mother, who was laid up with one of her worst headaches, who was a martyr to every variety

of nervous depression!—She would gladly
have been able to soothe and please her,
by bringing the intelligence for which she
longed so eagerly, and instead of this she
must carry to her news that would jar upon
her nerves, add to her pain, disappoint and
fret her, and perhaps do her serious injury!
How should she do it? Would it not have
been better to have done violence to her
feelings by promising to marry the man she
loathed than to have to be thus cruel to her
invalid mother? At least she was determined to postpone the evil day. She would
go off for a long ramble, leaving her mother
undisturbed until she was better fitted to
bear the news for which she would certainly
ask at the very earliest opportunity. She
glided lightly upstairs to prepare for her
walk; not so lightly, however, but that her
mother heard the gentle rustle of her dress:
and before she had reached her own room
a door was opened, a head thrust out, and
in shrilly-excited tones a voice called, "Margaret, Margaret, come here, my dear! I want
you,—I want to speak to you!"

There was nothing for it but to obey.

"What is it, mother, darling?" said Margaret, trying to speak naturally, and feeling smitten with remorse as she gazed at Mrs. Willoughby's pallid face, heavy eyes, and nervously twitching lips. "Please lie down again. You should not have called for me yourself; why didn't you ring the bell, and send for me through Jane?"

"I didn't want Jane," replied her mother, excitedly. "I wanted you. I want to know all that has passed between you and Miles this morning?"

"Miles?" returned Margaret, while she arranged her mother's pillows, and saw her settled on the bed. "Miles? Oh, you heard the door bell, then? Yes, he has been here this morning; but I thought I would tell you all about it by-and-by, when you are better. It will take so long, and you ought to be asleep, and I have things to do out of doors. Please, mother, let us talk about it comfortably, by-and-by, this evening, after tea?"

"Do you think I could get to sleep with

my mind in this state of suspense?" said
Mrs. Willoughby. "What nonsense, Margaret! Why can't you tell me at once
what answer you have given to him?"

"Oh, mother, I wish I could make you
know that he is not the good and delightful person he pretends to be! I wish I
could teach you to hate him, as I do!
Darling, I would do anything to please
you but this! Oh mother, if you could
but know what a detestable, odious humbug he is!"

"Margaret, be quiet!" screamed her
mother; "I won't have you speak another
word until you can speak more properly.
How dare you use such language about
a man who has done you the greatest
honour that a man can do to a woman! A
man, too, who could have any woman he
chose, all over the world, only for the asking!" She paused, breathless.

"Then, mother," said Margaret, with a
laugh, " he may the more easily console himself for my refusal of the offered honour!"

"You mean, then, to tell me that, knowing my wishes, knowing all our wishes, knowing all he has borne and done for your sake, the consideration he has shown to your feelings, the encouragement that you have given to him,—you actually dare to tell me that you have refused him altogether, without giving him a hope, without telling him that you will try to learn to love him? Margaret, I cannot believe that you have been so cruel, so selfish, so——"

"Mother, mother, you will hurt yourself, you will make yourself ill! Please, please, don't! If only you knew, you would not say all this. Let us talk about it by-and-by. Believe me I have given him no encouragement; if he told you I had, he—" she left the sentence unfinished, and turned away to the window to try to calm herself. She wanted only to think of her mother, to remember that she was ill and nervous, and not responsible for the cruel and unjust things that she had been saying; but it was hard not to feel aggrieved and hurt!

When she turned round again, Mrs.

Willoughby was sitting up, pressing one hand tightly down on the top of her head, and with the other clutching violently at the bed-clothes; and there was a look on her face which startled Margaret, and put everything but her mother's sufferings, for the moment, out of her head.

"Mother dear, lie down and let me bathe your forehead with *eau-de-cologne*," she said, soothingly.

But her mother signed her away.

"Go, Margaret, go," she exclaimed by-and-by, as Margaret continued to stand looking on in helpless trouble. "Go,—I am too ill to talk more now. Go,—you little know how much you have caused me to suffer!"

"Jane, you must go to mamma, please; she is very ill," said Margaret, abruptly, to the maid, on meeting her as she was leaving her mother's room.

And then she went out on the lawn, and walked about restlessly beneath the trees in front, looking up, from time to time, at Mrs. Willoughby's window, and, in her misery,

almost feeling inclined to vow any acqui-
escence in her mother's wishes, if only she
might be cured of her sufferings, and would
once more be pleased with her, and let her
nurse and caress her as usual.

CHAPTER XIII.

AND Miles? How was he bearing his share of misery all this time? How was he continuing to endure the disappointment of his life's best hopes? It would seem that he had found some one to help him to bear his burden,—to soothe him under the severe affliction which had befallen him! At the very moment when Margaret was out under the trees, alone with her great distress and anxiety, he who had caused them was to be seen sauntering slowly round a pleasant garden, at the back of Elgin Villa, near Darlingster, with a young lady whose name was Alice Craycroft. He looked at her tenderly. He spoke in low tones. And although he made her the *confidante* of his disappointed love, those looks and those tones seemed to belie his tale of woe. And

Alice, for the time being, was blissfully contented. It seemed to her that he was saying,—

"Circumstances have made it desirable that I should marry Margaret Willoughby, but my deepest affections are bestowed upon you, and it is to you that I look for comfort in my sorrow."

Not that he did say all this in so many words; but the momentary glances of his dark eyes suggested a thousand unutterable things, which Alice Craycroft's heart translated according to her own fond wishes. And in truth Miles Grantham found the society of this young lady fully as agreeable as that of Margaret Willoughby. Certainly she was not so clever, she was not so well-bred, she was not so naïve and graceful, she was not,—Miles in short, might have found a hundred negatives to the disadvantage of Alice Craycroft. But nevertheless, had the connection been equally good, had the fortune been equally sure, had the world smiled with equal approval on the one as on the other, it is probable that Alice's wistful looks, confiding ways, and flattering idolatry, would have gained a victory, and that poor Margaret might have been spared much worry, boredom, and more serious trouble. But as matters stood, pretty Alice Craycroft, with her vulgar relations and her boarding-school manners, was not deserving of a moment's serious thought on the part of so important a person as the heir of Grantham Hall. She might be put aside with a sigh, but put aside she must be. None the less for this, however, was it soothing to his vanity to be with her.

" Then you will write to me? You will not forget your promise?" he was saying now, as the *tête-à-tête* began to draw to a close? You will tell me all you can about her?"

" I will not forget. I will see as much of her as I can,—and I think,—I am almost certain,—that I shall have good news to send you," returned Alice, with a quiver in her voice, and with the sensation of being exceedingly generous and noble-minded, very like the heroine of one of her favourite novels. " But, but have you quite made up

your mind that it is best for you to go?
Perhaps if you were to stay, she might,—
oh, I am sure she could not help learning
to love you!"

He shook his head. "Ah, you do not
know her!" he answered. "Just now she
hates the very sight of me. No, I shall be
best away for the present. You judge
others by your own kind heart, Miss Craycroft!" She blushed and turned away.
The compliment was rather equivocal, but
the tone in which it was spoken, the look
with which it was accompanied, made it
thrill deliciously through Alice Craycroft's
sentimental soul. "But I shall come back
again, and perhaps try my luck once more,
one of these days," he went on, "and
if she continues to be cruel, at least I shall
know where to come for comfort. Miss
Craycroft, how can I thank you enough for
all your kindness!"

He was holding her hand in his, as he
spoke, and for an instant his timid eyes
gazed tenderly into hers.

"Good-bye, Miss Craycroft, good-bye, I

shall hear from you soon?" he continued, adding abruptly, as though with sudden recollection, "and you will remember to tell me if that old fellow Gilling annoys you again?"

"Oh, he did not annoy me. I was not at all frightened for myself. Only what he said struck me as very strange, and I felt as if I were living in a novel, and—and I thought perhaps I had better tell you."

"You were quite right, and I thank you very much, Miss Craycroft. I know you will kindly let it be a secret between you and me? Darlingster is such a gossiping place, and I would not have it come to my uncle's and aunt's ears for anything. It might disturb them. It does not trouble me in the least, but old people's minds are more easily upset. Gilling has been very strange for a long time. A year ago I thought that there was a screw loose about him, somewhere, and it is very evident to me now that he is fast going out of his mind."

"Really!" exclaimed Alice, with an air of alarm.

"Oh, you need not be frightened, Miss Craycroft. There is no fear of his becoming violent. But he must be watched. I mean to keep an eye upon him, quietly. And you will help me?"

"Oh, yes, yes," answered Alice eagerly.

"It was yesterday, you say, that you saw him, and that he said what you told me?"

"Yes; I went to the cottage when it got cool enough for walking, and when I knew he would be back from his work. He began by telling me that you had come, and how good you had been to him, and then,—yes, certainly I noticed that he got very odd and excited."

"Ah!" returned Miles, thoughtfully, "I see. I must be more careful! Good-bye, Miss Craycroft. I shall hope to hear soon, then, good-bye," and so they squeezed hands, and parted.

Alice watched him out of sight, the delightful sense of being a mover in an actual romance growing upon her as she did so. She had often envied Margaret, but she envied her no longer; she only pitied her bad taste. "He will awake from his dreams all in good time!" she said to herself. "He will find out the meaning of his tender feeling for me. And we shall laugh together over his old fancied love for her. Of course, though, I shall try to make her love him. I must be generous, and sacrifice my own feelings for their sakes, if needful! But I don't think,—I scarcely think,—she can care for him. If she does, if I sacrifice myself and bring them together, I shall certainly go into a decline! They will watch me gradually fading away, and as soon as I am gone he will find out that it was me whom he loved all the time! Alas, poor Miles!"

The sad vision that she had conjured up seemed so interesting, that for a few moments she thought it would be almost as good a reality as that of a happy marriage. But those few moments past, her fears of disappointment became very active.

"I think I'll look in upon her this evening," she thought, "after he has left, and find out what her feeling really is. And I'll go and see that old man; perhaps he will say something more curious. It may be ne-

cessary for me to write to Mr. Grantham
to-morrow;" which delightful contingency
made Alice happy for the present. Miles had
for once spoken the truth when he had talked
of the gossiping tendencies of the people of
Darlingster. But he was not aware that in
all the neighbourhood no one loved gossip
better than Alice herself. Her soul delighted
in it, and with gossip as the object in view,
she was an indefatigable visitor, both of rich
and poor. She had had a double motive,
however, in visiting old Gilling on the previous afternoon. She had heard of Miles
Grantham's arrival at the Hall, and had
gone to see his *protégé*, as she considered old
Gilling, in the hope of an encounter with
himself; or, failing this, on the chance of
learning something about him. It is possible,
also, that his meeting with the heir of Grantham, accompanied with an order to go and
drink his health, may have had something to
do with the gardener's excitement and want
of reticence during her visit, and that Miles
may have been wise in his present resolution
to be more careful for the future. At all

events, Alice had found little difficulty in drawing Gilling into an engrossing gossip about the Hall and its inhabitants, and he had been considerably more gracious and more confidential with her than was in accordance with his usual noted reserve.

Her resolve to renew her visit to Grantham that evening was carried out; but with disappointing results. The old gardener was surly, and would not enlarge on any topic that was brought forward. And if she did get anything out of him in reference to Grantham Hall, it was of a most matter-of-fact and every-day nature, and seemed to contradict his mysterious words of the evening before. She almost began to think that the revelation that had been made to her was only part of a strange and unaccountable dream, and that actual life was not so romantic a thing as her impressions of the last twenty-four hours had led her to hope. On leaving Gilling, she went to The Cottage, but was dismayed to learn that Mrs. Willoughby was exceedingly ill, and that Miss Willoughby could see nobody.

CHAPTER XIV.

WE left Margaret anxiously looking up at her mother's window, from beneath the trees on The Cottage lawn. It seemed an endless watch. Half an hour or so went by, and still Jane was to be seen gliding about the bedroom or standing by the bedside. Presently a bell rang, and soon afterwards Margaret heard the hall-door being opened and shut, and discovered that Jane was leaving the sick room. She hastened indoors, and upstairs, just as some one was being ushered in to her mother. Then having waylaid Jane, she was informed that Lady Grantham was with Mrs. Willoughby.

"Lady Grantham! But mamma was not fit to see any one!" exclaimed Margaret.

"It was her wish, miss. I wasn't to say anything to nobody. I was to send for Lady

Grantham immediate. I don't know as it will do any good, but the mischief is already done."

"Mischief, Jane? What mischief? Is there much the matter?" asked Margaret, in alarm.

"I never see her so bad before; I should say some one had been bothering of her," answered Jane, severely.

"Had we not better send for Mr. Thomas?" said Margaret.

"It ain't doctors what'll do her any good, miss; it's some one what'll consider her feelings, and not worrit her by their contrariness."

"I don't think you understand much about it, Jane," replied Margaret, trying to assume some dignity with her mother's confidential maid. What has mamma been saying?"

"Enough to make me understand more than you think, perhaps, Miss Margaret. Any one as has got troubles and sufferings must come out to *some* one as has feelings. It's well for them if they've got *any* one as can sympathise with them! Poor dear

missis! She does suffer terrible, to be
sure!"

"What is that?" cried Margaret, suddenly. "How odd mamma's voice sounds!
Jane, do go in, and see if she is any worse."

"Don't you fidget, Miss Margaret. I
know when to go in, and I ain't going to put
myself forward, until the time comes."

"Then I shall go in," said Margaret.

" But this the autocrat of the bedchamber
peremptorily forbade; and having thus as-
serted her self-importance, Jane hastened
without further delay, to Mrs. Willoughby's
room; while Margaret stationed herself at
the door, and listened, in an agony, to groans
and rambling talk, and soothing replies.

Presently Jane came out, and said,
hurriedly, "She's off her head, poor dear;
talks all of a *incoherient* fashion, what it's
awful to hear. Them as has done it has a
deal to answer for! We must send for the
doctor immediate; but *I* can't leave her,
poor dear."

Margaret took the hint, and a messenger
was sent without delay into Darlingster for

the doctor, who soon appeared, and pronounced it to be a case of nervous fever.
He came out with Lady Grantham, looking
very grave; and Margaret felt two pairs of
eyes gazing reproachfully at her, while he
talked of "disturbing causes," "an excitable
nature," "sensitive nerves," "hysteria" and
so forth.

She could not have felt much more remorseful or miserable than she felt at that
moment had she known herself to have been
her mother's wilful murderer. What did it
matter to her that she had not intentionally
injured her mother, and that it had grieved
her to the heart to have to vex her? She *had*
vexed her, she, her child, had been the cause
of her illness! So she angrily told herself.
A thousand exaggerated fears came over her,
and when Lady Grantham returned to her
mother's room, she ran downstairs just in
time to catch the doctor before he went out
at the hall door.

" Is mamma very ill, Mr. Thomas ? " she
asked, breathlessly. "Is there any danger?"

Perhaps an inkling of something allied to

the true state of the case came to the good
man, as he looked at the eager face that was
anxiously raised to his.   That noble brow,
those sweet eyes, and that tender mouth did
not look as if they ought to belong to a
vixenish and unmanageable daughter !   He
saw, at least, that she had been needlessly
alarmed, and he re-assured her with kindly
looks and words.

" She must be kept very quiet.   She must
not be annoyed or troubled in any way.
And then, with the help of your good nurs-
ing, Miss Willoughby, I hope we shall soon
see her herself again," were his last words.

Relieved and thankful, Margaret took her
way upstairs, and, in spite of Jane's forbid-
ding looks, dared to enter her mother's room.
" I am going to stay here," she whispered,
seating herself in a low chair, at the head
of the bed, where she was hidden by the
curtain.   " Mr. Thomas says I may, so you
can go down and have your dinner, Jane."

" I ain't a-going to leave missis, Miss
Margaret.   So it's no use your saying nothing about it."

" Yes you are, Jane, and I'll be sure to ring if we want anything."

So having delivered her soul of a protest, Jane found it convenient to go. Then Lady Grantham, looking at her watch, said she was afraid she must not remain any longer, adding, in a freezing tone, " You will be sure to let me know, Margaret, if your poor mamma should be worse, if there should be any change, or if she should ask for me? And I hope you will be careful not to disturb her by any painful allusions. Mr. Thomas says he will not answer for the consequences if she is worried or thwarted in the slightest degree. She seems to have fallen into a doze now,—sleep is her best chance, but I don't like her look at all."

With which cheering observation Lady Grantham went away, and Margaret was left to her own reflections. Amidst all her anxiety and distress, she found herself longing, more passionately than she had ever longed before, for Charles Meredith. If she might only see him for a moment, tell him all about it, ask his advice and receive his sympathy, she thought she could bear anything almost that might be about to happen ! If he would only come again, her mother would see that he was sincere, would soften towards him, would learn to love him, and to hate Miles, would recover, and, in short, all would be right ! In the quiet of the sick room, Margaret almost dreamed herself, for a while, back into happiness.

CHAPTER XV.

THE world of Darlingster and its neighbourhood was very busy for a time with the
affairs of the inhabitants of Grantham
Cottage, in connection with Grantham Hall.
"That flirt Margaret" came in for a large
share of blame. People talked of her ill-
treatment of Miles: of how she had given
him as much encouragement as it was possible for a girl to give, of how she had cast
her spells over him, drawing him away from
others, at whose feet he would otherwise
have thrown himself,—all for the sake of
feeding her own vanity. Some one even
hinted at mysterious reasons for this with-
drawal of her favour from Miles. And
there were not wanting those who expressed doubts as to whether it was, after
all, so certain as had been supposed that

it was Sir John Grantham's intention to leave the property to his nephew. In short, a thousand extravagant notions were being bruited about. But the more moderate and sober-minded gossips put down these rumours as the chimerical and romantic fancies of an extreme party; and were content, for their part, with the belief that Margaret's bad behaviour had almost broken a good man's heart, and had well-nigh driven a tender and solicitous mother out of her mind or into her coffin. Many heads were shaken over Mrs. Willoughby's illness. Some doubted whether she would ever rise from her bed again. Others declared it to be impossible that her mind could ever recover its proper balance. And it was generally given out that she was laid up with a severe attack of brain fever.

Margaret, meanwhile, had the satisfaction of seeing her mother gradually improve in health. She was soon able to sit up, and before long Mr. Thomas pronounced her to be convalescent. But, unfortunately, Mrs. Willoughby's opinion did not tally with that of her doctor. And long after he had given her permission to go out, and had assured Margaret that there was no longer any cause for anxiety, she considered herself to be unfit to move from her room, and wondered that the doctor should be so foolish as to pretend to think her better, when he must know that she had come to a standstill, and was not likely to recover even the little strength that she had had before her terrible illness.

Again and again the nervous invalid almost succeeded in frightening her daughter out of her wits, and Margaret was hardly reassured by the doctor's own assertion,— which she wonderingly overheard one day, when his tones were raised somewhat higher than their wont, during a confidential conver-sation with Jane, not far from her mistress's door.

"She might be as strong as anybody," he said, "if she chose! She only wants to recover her nervous energy, which she will never do until she allows herself some fresh air, and begins to exert herself a little."

When Margaret went to her mother, with some notion of cheering her up, with a modification of the doctor's opinion, she found her walking quickly about the room, in great excitement, and with as much ease as if she did not know what weakness meant. She was crying and sobbing hysterically, and after a moment's pause of dismayed astonishment, Margaret hastened to give her a glass of camphor julep. But she signed her away.

"No," she panted; "no,"—then came a great gulp,—"I don't want it, I don't want anything. Let me die, and then you will have no more trouble with me, and can disobey my wishes as much as you like!"

"Mother dear, what in the world do you mean? Mr. Thomas says you are better, and that it would do you good to go out. He would laugh at the notion of your dying."

To Margaret's surprise, this cheering news only occasioned a fresh burst of tears.

"I see what it is,—I see what it is! You have been making out to Mr. Thomas that

I give way, that I could do a great deal more if I liked;" so she jerked out, between spasmodic attacks of weeping and panting. "He shall see,—he shall see! I will exert myself as much as you all wish, and it won't matter if it kills me. You will be rid of the trouble of me."

"Mother, darling, don't! How can you say such horrible things? You know quite well that I should not care for my life at all if I had not you to think about. Do lie down and rest; you will wear yourself out!"

"I am not going to lie down. I am going out. Tell Jane to come and get my walking things out for me. It is all very well, Margaret, for you to call me darling, and to pretend in words to be very affec-tionate and dutiful. But you know well enough that that will do me no good while you continue obstinately determined to rebel against my wishes. It all depends upon you whether or not I regain my health and strength. You know well enough what caused my illness in the first instance; and how do you think I am ever to get well if my mind continues to be troubled and harassed in the same manner? "

" Mamma, you know that I long to please you. I will try, indeed I will, to do all that you wish," Here she paused abruptly, for at the moment Jane entered.

" Well, my dear child, we will talk about this again by-and-by," said Mrs. Willoughby, brightening up. And, her agitation somewhat calmed, she sank down in an easy chair, nearly exhausted by her late unwonted efforts.

" Mamma wants you to get her ready to go out," said Margaret; " but I think she ought to rest and have a glass of wine before she goes."

" She ain't no more fit to go out and walk nor a baby," said Jane; "I don't care if a hundred doctors says she is." But Mrs. Willoughby was bent on martyrdom. She would not even have a carriage. She chose to go and walk herself tired, and came in with a splitting headache. Then in the evening she chose to agitate herself.

" Margaret," she said, with startling

suddenness, "will you promise to try to love Miles Grantham ? "

"Mamma dear ! " cried Margaret, in dismayed as astonishment. "What can I say? How can I try? What can I do? Let me think over what you ask, and we can talk about it another time. You must try to get to sleep now ; Mr. Thomas likes you to go to bed early."

"I understand, I know !" cried her mother, shrilly. "Very well, Margaret, deceive me as you did before ! Make me ill again ! Consult your own wishes before those of your mother ! "

"Mother, darling, don't say such cruel things," said Margaret, beseechingly. "You know well enough how I love you. It is only because you are tired that you think so hardly of me."

"Very well, very well, say no more about it ; I won't hear another word on the subject, to-night! Only, Mr. Thomas must know what it is that retards my recovery, and makes a slight exertion upset my nerves so terribly. Oh, if you had ever felt such suffering as this!" And she pressed her hand on the top of her head, and closed her eyes, and put on an expression of martyr-like submission. In short, Mrs Willoughby had made up her mind to resign herself to interesting invalidism for the rest of her life, unless,—unless she could have her own way,—unless her present whim with regard to her daughter could be satisfied! She had the satisfaction of finding herself much worse the next morning. "Ah," she thought, "Mr. Thomas will have to own now that I am not fit for the least exertion. He will see to-day how really ill I am!" And certainly he did find her nervously feverish, and looking very un-well. She was evidently suffering much.

"Your orders was attended to, sir," said Jane, in a tone of asperity. "And missis went out to walk yesterday.

"You shouldn't have let her over do it," retorted the doctor.

"Missis has such *h*energy, you see, sir, it ain't easy to keep her within bounds!"

"I find a very little knocks me up, at present," said Mrs. Willoughby, languidly.

"You must go on, by degrees, doing a little bit more each day," said the doctor. "You are certainly not fit for anything to-day but to lie still; but I hope in a day or two we may get you out on the lawn for a few minutes' fresh air."

"It ain't fresh air what missis wants," said Jane, when, his say ended, she followed the doctor to the door; and a sob from the bed at the same moment made both turn round to look again at the invalid. "She've a deal to trouble her," went on Jane, in a low tone, "and them as does it has a deal to answer for!" And then she added something in a whisper.

After his parley with the lady's-maid, Mr. Thomas went to the drawing-room in search of Margaret.

"My dear Miss Willoughby," he said, "you really must take care not to agitate your mamma in any way. Her nerves, as you know, are not in a state to bear it. I find her suffering very much to-day from having been upset yesterday."

Margaret looked distressed.

"I know," she answered, "and I thought I had tried not to let her be worried. But I am afraid I manage very badly."

"You mean that she is easily disturbed and distressed? Or has she something especial on her mind, which she cannot forget?"

His manner was so kind, so little impertinent, as he asked these questions, that Margaret felt half inclined to come out to him with her troubles, and to ask his advice and help.

"I don't know what Lady Grantham and our maid may have said to you," she replied; "but perhaps you ought to know that their *is* something that is troubling poor mamma. I have disappointed her about something. I cannot quite explain it to you, but,—I don't know how to help vexing her without being untrue. And of course now that she is so ill, she feels it doubly."

"It is very hard for you, my dear," said Mr. Thomas; "but it is really of the utmost importance that your mamma should not be agitated at present. You must avoid the painful subject as far as possible ; and you must contrive to give in to her wishes just now as much as you can."

" More easily said than done ! " Margaret thought; but the doctor was so serious, and frightened her so much by the way in which he talked of her mother's nervous state, and the mental consequences to be feared if her wishes were injudiciously opposed, that she resolved to exercise all the tact and ingenuity that she could command, to put her own feelings on one side, let her mother feel that she was studying hers, gain peace and quiet for the present, and leave the future to take care of itself.

Meanwhile, in spite of the orders that he had given, Mr. Thomas' sympathies were with Margaret, and not with his patient; and as he left the house, he determined to be on the look out, and to take good care that the poor child was not bullied by that weak and selfish mother, and her foolish friends. But with all his good intentions, what could the kind-hearted man do to help Margaret out of her troubles? Nothing

as yet, at any rate. His advice was followed. His patient got better. And all
for a time appeared to go smoothly. But
Margaret was still, secretly, often troubled,
anxious, and heavy-hearted.

CHAPTER XV.

A DECIDED change for the better had been effected in Mrs. Willoughby's health, and it was Margaret who had applied the remedy! She had promised her mother to bear again with the society and the attentions of Miles Grantham, to permit him to use every effort to win her, and even to try to conquer her own seemingly un-conquerable aversion. She had not stayed to count the cost. The desire to save her mother from farther pain,—the hope of seeing her cheerful and well,—had been strong enough to overcome all other thought and feeling. So the weak and wilful woman was able to victimise her loving child. A con-versation between Lady Grantham and Mrs. Willoughby had resulted in the despatch of a letter to Miles, recalling him to Grant-

ham. He had arrived. A series of little
parties had been instituted at the Hall.
Mrs. Willoughby had suddenly recovered
sufficient strength to enable her to enjoy
the pleasures of society up to a tolerably
late hour at night. And all went gaily as
a marriage feast. Even Margaret,—in spite
of the irksomeness of her position, as the
adored of Miles, in spite of her secret mis-
giving as to how the drama in which she
was taking a part was to end,—found the
relief from her late nightmare fears and her
past distress, on her mother's account, so
great, that it was very possible for her, also,
to be very heartily merry. Her mother
looked on approvingly, and for the present,
at least, her sacrifice was not without its
reward. She really succeeded in being
passably civil to Miles. And though the
unnecessary amount of languor and irritabi-
lity, and the persistent invalid habits, which
daylight always seemed to bring back to the
nervous patient, were somewhat trying to
her daughter, she bore all with as much
equaminity as possible, and really did her

best to be amiable and cheerful. Only,
when the need for immediate effort was
over, and she was alone,—without excitement, and without the eyes of a gossiping
world upon her,—she gave herself up to
perplexing and troublous thoughts, and
to sore longings, which seemed as if they
must have some result.

Again and again she echoed the question,
" How is it all to end?" "I am a great
humbug," she thought to herself,—"I am
a great humbug, I am afraid. For though
I certainly don't give Miles any encouragement, I fear I am buoying mamma up with
hopes which can never be fulfilled, without
my becoming a worse humbug, and perhaps
breaking other hearts besides my own. How
will she bear the disappointment at last!
and would any other heart be broken ?
Does he care still " ?

A great leap at her heart would seem to
answer "Yes," and then her grave reflections
would often be concluded by a laugh, and a
declaration to herself that there was nothing
for it but putting on the spirit of a Micawber,

and waiting, philosophically, for "something
to turn up." "Something surely, surely must
turn up! It is impossible that we can go on
in this miserable manner for ever." Thus
her thoughts would often run, youthful hope
getting the better of gloomy forebodings.

But the winter came, without anything
"turning up" to alter the current of Margaret's life. There was the usual house-full
at the Hall, for Christmas. There were the
usual balls and dinner parties at Darlingster.
Miles Grantham continued to appear pecu-
liarly attentive to each young lady of the
neighbourhood, to be extraordinarily tender
to Alice Craycroft, and to be serious in his
devotion to Margaret Willoughby. He was
in no hurry to marry, and the present state
of affairs suited his inclinations remarkably
well; especially as he agreed with Lady
Grantham that there could be no doubt
whatever of his final success. Margaret
continued to submit to Miles' persecution, for
her mother's sake, with as good a grace as
she could. And Mrs. Willoughby continued
to approve, complain, hope, and despair by

turns, and, through all, to determine, strongly, to have her own way, and to permit her daughter to be happy in no other.

Spring came and went; but the something that was expected " to turn up" might be looked for in vain.

Summer arrived, and Mrs. Willoughby showed visible signs of impatience, and even threatened to invite the attack of another nervous fever, if Margaret waited much longer without throwing herself into the arms of Miles Grantham.

Mr. Thomas was called in to ward off, if he could, the expected illness. But to Mrs. Willoughby's aggrieved surprise, he gave more heed to Margaret's pale cheeks and looks of weariness than he did to her own nervous symptoms. Change of air was prescribed for Margaret, and small attention paid to her own protest that it was unnecessary, or to her mother's declaration that she could not stand the fatigue of travelling, and could not possibly spare Margaret, now that she was on the verge of a feverish illness.

" It was a cruel world," Mrs. Willoughby

thought, "a cruel and unsympathizing world!" All her objections were beaten down, and there was "no one but poor Jane to understand" her! An opportunely pressing invitation to London, however, came to settle the question. Mrs. Willoughby was excited into forgetfulness of her threatened illness, and thought she should like to go. She had always been too indolent to give Margaret the chance of amusement in town, during the season; but going on a visit to a luxurious house was a different matter. She would be spared all trouble, and could go out, or not go out, as the fancy took her, or as her health permitted. Besides, there was the chance that Margaret might marry Lord Any-Body, which, after all, would be as good or even better than, as, marrying the heir of Grantham; or, at any rate, she might learn to forget that stupid young nobody who had chosen to fall in love with her, and things might be brought to a point with Miles Grantham, who had loved her so long and so devotedly.

For herself, Margaret was ready to wel-

come any change that would distract her
mother's mind from its usual favourite subjects of contemplation, Miles Grantham and
nervous fever. And besides, who could
tell what happy occurrences might not take
place during the London visit! She did
not know what she expected,—in fact she
expected nothing in particular; but anything was possible, anything might turn up,
to throw glowing colours over her own life
and her mother's.

So the invitation was accepted, and its
acceptance resulted in new whims and new
hopes for Mrs. Willoughby, and in new
worries for her daughter Margaret! Not
that the visit was by any means made up of
worry for Margaret: far otherwise! She
enjoyed it for a time intensely. The sights
and sounds and society of London amused
and interested her fresh and eager mind.
Her enjoyment, moreover, was in a manner
double, for as she recalled past conversa-
tions with Charles Meredith, on pictures,
music, and people, and fancied what he
would say with reference to this or that

person or thing, she seemed to be drawn nearer to him in spirit, and to be able to enter, through her imagination, into all his thoughts, feelings, and opinions. Excitement, too, had the power of quickening her hopes. It was impossible, she thought, utterly impossible, but that she must be meant to meet him again before long !

There were moments, however, when she gazed with heart-sick, hopeless longings through the crowd, in search of the one face which it would have been sweet to her to see. And there were weary moments of re-action after excitement, when her heart ached sorely after the friend whom she loved so well, and when her inner life seemed all the more dreary to her for the outward pleasures and gaiety in which she had been taking a part.

"Mother dear, when are we going home?" asked Margaret, rather wearily, one night when bed-time had arrived, after a dinner-party at the house of the friends with whom they were staying.

"Home, Margaret ! Are you not happy

here? Do you want to go home? I
thought you seemed happy enough this
evening, when you were talking to Lord
Mark Denham!" answered her mother,
rather sharply.

"Yes, mamma, I like him very much," said
Margaret, thinking to herself how especially
she had felt to like him when it had acci-
dentally come out that Charles Meredith had
been an Oxford friend of his, and he had
mentioned having met him some months
since, in the Louvre at Paris ;—and remembering the heart-sinking disappointment she
had felt on finding that he had nothing to
tell her about his old friend's present life
and whereabouts. "Do you know, mamma,
she added, with sudden impulse, "he knows
Mr. Meredith! They were acquaintances at
Oxford, and he liked him immensely."

"Indeed," returned Mrs. Willoughby,
coldly, and with an irritating smile; "and is
it this interesting reminder of Mr. Meredith
that has given you the wish to withdraw
from the world, and retire into the seclusion
of Grantham all of a sudden?"

" Mamma, what nonsense!" answered Margaret, quickly. " I beg your pardon, but did you fancy that I had forgotten Mr. Meredith, so soon? We were too close friends, and saw far too much of each other, for that to be possible. But you need not be afraid of my speaking of him as anything more than a great friend. Perhaps he has left off thinking about me; at any rate, I do not expect him to come in search of me, so you may make yourself quite easy, mother, on the subject of Charles Meredith."

" Then, my love, I cannot understand why you should have got tired of this pleasant life so quickly. If Miles Grantham were at home, now——"

" You can scarcely think, mamma," broke in Margaret, with some impatience, " that that thought would make me long to find myself at home again."

" My dear child," said Mrs. Willoughby, the notion suddenly jumping into her head, " can it be possible that, that— Have you been disappointed in any way about Lord Mark Denham? Has he—is he——"

"Disappointed about Lord Mark Denham? What in the world can you mean,
mother?" laughed Margaret. "What
could happen to disappoint me about Lord
Mark Denham? Lord Mark and I are very
good friends, but we are in no way deeply
interested in each other's life and welfare."

"Margaret, Margaret," said Mrs. Willoughby, reproachfully, "will you ever learn
not to trifle with other people's affections in
this heartless, cruel manner! I tell you, if
ever man was attached to woman, Lord
Mark Denham is attached to you!"

"Mamma!" began Margaret.

But her mother went on,—

"And you pretend to tell me that you
mean nothing by all the apparent encouragement that you have given him?"

"If to answer a civil question with a
civil answer is to give encouragement, I am
guilty of having given Lord Mark Denham
whatever encouragement he may desire,
supposing that to be any. I don't know in
what other way I can have appeared to give
him encouragement."

"My dear, it is of no use for you to deny that Lord Mark Denham is continually at your side, talking to you, whispering to you, and paying you every sort of marked attention. Your cousin Mary observed it as well as I. Margaret, will you ever learn to know you own mind? We thought the other day that you seemed to be completely engrossed by Sir Thomas Fletcher, but his going out of town seemed not to affect you in the slightest degree, and now,—oh, I did hope that it was going to be all right with poor Lord Mark Denham."

"And so it will be all right for him, depend upon it, mamma!" returned Margaret, laughing, while she rang the bell for Jane, and turned to leave her mother's room.

"I can't make you out, Margaret!" said Mrs. Willoughby, plaintively. "It seems to me that you are never satisfied. I hoped that you had been enjoying yourself since we came up to town. You have appeared happy enough, and now it turns out that all the time you have been longing to be at home again."

"Indeed you are mistaken, mother. I have enjoyed myself immensely, and shall be contented to stay here as much longer as you like. Only I got just now a sort of craving for a sight of the wood and a breath of home air."

"Ah, we will have Lord Mark Denham down to see our woods!" said Mrs. Willoughby, brightening up; and she added, to herself, "I am determined, at all events, to put an end to the girl's dreaming about that young Mr. Meredith."

CHAPTER XVI.

The London season came to a close. The Willoughbys returned home, to be congratulated on the good which change of air and gaiety had effected. And Margaret found it very easy to be bright, to talk glibly of her gay time in London, and with interest of all that she had seen and done. She felt indeed to have gained something. Fresh windows had been opened in her mind, and she was able to live, as it were, new lives, apart from her own peculiar life and its concerns.

The people at the Hall congratulated Mrs. Willoughby on the improvement in her daughter. They were convinced that London had cured her of her dreamy fancies about young Meredith. Lady Grantham was glad that "the child had had her chance," and as, apparently, she had come

back heart-whole, she had a better hope than
ever that her dear Miles would finally succeed in winning her. He was coming down
soon, and, somehow, Margaret bore the
prospect of his visit better than she had
ever borne it before. She felt, instinctively,
that her mother's " views " for her had
widened and multiplied ; and this feeling
lessened the sense of *géne* with which she
had always contemplated the approaching
presence of Miles Grantham.

But below all this increase of freedom and
relief, below all this fresh sunshine which
had crept unawares over the surface of her
life, lay a sense of blank and disappointment,
which often caused her heart to ache
heavily. The hopes which she had carried
with her to town had been very vague and
indefinite ; but now that the excitement
which had given them life had passed away,
it seemed to her that the one thing for
which she had really cared had died with
them, and had left her innermost soul coldly
dreary and desolate. Mrs. Willoughby
might have accused her, with justice, of

dreaming about Charles Meredith. And as she wandered through the woods, indulging melancholy and morbid musings, she asked herself, "What more is to come? Is this wretched state of things to go on for ever and ever? Am I never to see him,—never to explain?"

The sudden mention of him, the slight information about him, had been just enough to tantalize her, and to make her fancies about him more tangible, and the longings to clear away the misunderstanding with which he had left her more intense. The momentary bliss of hearing him spoken of had left her more heart-hungry than she had been before, and there was apparently no chance of her hunger being ever satisfied.

By-and-by, however, the effect of reaction after excitement passed away, and she gave herself up with more healthy energy to the quiet interests of her useful home life. By-and-by, too, she began to say to herself again, "Something, surely, will throw a light yet! Who knows what another year may bring about?" "Hope on, hope ever,"

was once more the motto which made the
pleasant burden of her youthful song !

How would it end? What would "throw
a light?" Was the quiet history of the
daily life which seemed to her so colourless
and so unromantic, being woven by unseen
hands into a chain of events which were
closely connected with the secret story of
her inmost heart? Were the common-place
beings who lived and moved around her,
acting a part which would prove them here-
after to have been, in truth, characters moving upon the scenes of her own Life's Drama?
Would anything that had power to touch
her very nearly ever come to change delight-
fully the tenour of her life? or would she only
learn, gradually, to be reconciled to things
as they were?—to see the history of her days
by degrees harmonizing into meaning and
beauty?—to see even disappointments and
troubles, and things unexplained, changed
by some mysterious and gracious agency
into a marvellous net-work of lovely colouring,
formed of submission, gentleness, strength
patient hope, and loving sympathy?

CHAPTER XVII.

EIGHT years had passed away since the night on which Miles Grantham had interrupted a *tête-à-tête* between Charles Meredith and Margaret Willoughby. Eight years had passed, and Charles Meredith had not yet crossed Margaret's path again! She had given up expecting it! She had given up "expecting something to happen." She had given up looking back with a lingering, longing, passionate gaze, that would fain have dispelled the bitterness of a "faultful past," and have drawn its sweetness up into the living present. She had given up looking into the far future with impatient, restless eyes, that would fain have shaped the shadowy distance according to the fashion of their "own sweet will."

Years of uncertainty had taught her a

lesson of certainty! She had become reconciled to the imperfections of her life, and
had learnt to find it sweet and dear, despite
its many faults. She no longer hungered
after her former friend and companion, but ·
she had not lost her faith in him. She had
not given up the hope that, some time,
—in some mysterious way (who could
tell how, or when, or where?),—she should
find herself with him again, loving him, and
being loved, with a love that was the better
and the truer for all these years of separation
and waiting. Could she at this instant have
seen Charles Meredith, would her dreams
have been dispelled? Would she have
found the reality answering to the noble
ideal which had so long dwelt in the world
of her imagination? However this may
have been, it is certain that if the real
Charles Meredith was possessed of powers
of appreciation equalling those of the hero
of Margaret's dreams, he would have found
the Margaret Willoughby of the present day
no less deserving of his admiration, or of
his love, than she had been in the days of

her early youth. She had lost nothing, and she had gained much. What had been bright about her had become softer in its brilliant light, what had been soft and gentle, had gained in strength, what had been sweet was more bewitchingly and surprisingly sweet than it had been before! And over her movements, or the lines of her face and figure when in repose, there rested an indefinable grace, which implied an absence of egoism and self-consciousness, and gave, even to a passing beholder, the sense of a true and tender sympathy. Anyone who was hunting the world for a faultless woman would certainly have been disappointed in Margaret Willoughby; but he who, stumbling upon her unawares, failed to be satisfied with her imperfection, must indeed have been of a nature difficult to please, and hypercritical in the last extreme. At the present moment, however, she might have been painted as a picture rather of Perfection than of Imperfection. It was a still August afternoon. The shadows were lengthening across the lawn,

while the golden sunshine lay in brilliant
contrast by their side, or crept stealthily
through the thick foliage of trees and
shrubs, or slanted quietly across ivy-covered
stems and trunks. And Margaret's attitude,
as she rested beneath the branches of a wide-
spreading cedar tree, harmonised with the
scene around, and expressed the perfection
of repose and of unconscious grace. Her
musings, too, were in accordance with the
peaceful atmosphere. She was in a halcyon
mood, troubled by no thought of evil,
desiring and fearing no change; simply
feeling that existence, in the abstract, was a
very pleasant and lovely possession; or if a
disturbing thought, or a wish for change,
crossed her mind, it was the thought of her
mother's ill health, and the wish that she
knew how to soothe away her pain and
depression, and to chime in more helpfully
with all her nervous fancies. As a whole,
her thoughts were no less bright and peaceful than they might have been on a like
beautiful summer's day eight years before.
And if she had mused on the outward

changes that had taken place in the parish
of Grantham, during those eight years, she
would have found little to disturb her peace
of mind. Sir John and Lady Grantham
were kind as ever, and a slight increase of
grey amidst the hairs on their heads did
not destroy the geniality of their appearance.
A few deaths and marriages had taken
place in the village. The rector was easy-
going, good-humoured, and broad-chested
as formerly. Old Gilling had become more
feeble, but was as fond of muttering as of
yore, and Margaret was still often amused
by his quaint remarks, or frightened by his
dark looks and strange vague hints at some
guilty mystery, or unfulfilled promise, which
was weighing heavily upon his mind.

Alice Craycroft was still unmarried, and,
moreover, frequently avowed with a gentle
sigh, that it was her firm intention to lead a
life of single blessedness. Her true hopes
and fears on this subject were kept religiously
to herself. Sometimes, to quote her own expressions in soliloquy, she was " consumed by
a burning jealousy ! " Sometimes she was

"wafted high on the wings of hopeful love!" She frequently visited old Gillings' cottage, tried to be intimate with Margaret, and succeeded in being so with the lady's-maid. She kept up a tolerably brisk correspondence with Mr. Grantham, gleaning for him all the information she could with reference to Margaret's many admirers, relating incidents connected with her experiences when out visiting in town, or elsewhere, and even transcribing scraps out of letters which Margaret supposed to have been seen by no eyes but her own, and perhaps her mother's, and innocently imagined to be possessed of no interest to anyone else connected with the neighbourhood. The tender correspondent, however, always concluded with a prayer that Mr. Grantham would keep up his spirits, for she was "sure, quite sure," in spite of appearances, that "dear Margaret" was "true at heart," and could not fail to love him as he deserved to be loved, in time!

Miles Grantham still paid frequent visits to the Hall, and had not relinquished his

purpose of winning Margaret Willoughby's
hand. But Margaret bore the tedium of
his presence and of his attentions with
greater equanimity than formerly. She knew
better how to hold her own, and told herself
that it was wiser to let things take their
course, and weary themselves to death, than
to fret and fume and fuss at the tiresome
eccentricities of a provoking and benighted
world.

On this particular afternoon, however, she
was not so much as troubled by a passing
thought of an uncongenial outer world, or
of the differences of opinion entertained, on
certain subjects, by herself and her elders.
She was giving herself up completely to
the luxury of undisturbed repose, rejoice-
ing in the knowledge that no callers were
likely to invade the premises, because all
Darlingster was engaged to a grand afternoon party; and other neighbours, even
including the Granthams, were absent from
home.

A green-backed volume of poetry lay on
the grass by her side. She idly turned its

pages, wondering, though with placid contentment, how soon her mother would fulfil
her promise to come out of doors, for the
agreed-upon reading of Tennyson.

Poor Margaret! More things than were
dreamed of in her pleasant summer day's
philosophy were already being discussed
as known facts by the much excited gossips
of Darlingster. All Darlingster knew what
the four o'clock train had brought fourth
in the shape of a visitor for The Cottage!
All Darlingster knew the meaning of the
carriage-wheels which were rolling with due
speed along the high road from Darlingster
to Grantham. And while Margaret was
resting in blissful forgetfulness that change
or disturbance could find a place on the
earth, the Darlingster mind was travelling
with amazing rapidity over the numberless
changes and counter-changes which would
doubtless be brought about by the present
brilliant chance which had turned up trumps
for the lucky Margaret Willoughby!

It was not long, however, before the low
songs of contentment which were making

melody in her heart, were interrupted by the sound of those very carriage-wheels which had been the cause of so much interest and excitement to her neighbours at Darlingster. A loud ringing at the door-bell quickly followed, as a climax of discomfiture.

"Who in the world can it be?" she thought. "Must I go in? or will it be only some manageable old lady, whom mamma can conveniently entertain without my aid? Who *can* it be? The carriage has gone, and mamma has come down, and, oh, dear, dear, she is beckoning to me, and I suppose I must go! Bother the person!"

The "person" proved to be a pleasant visitor, much liked by Margaret herself. But there was a flutter of suppressed excitement in Mrs. Willoughby's voice, and a simpering smile on her face, while she said,—

"Margaret, my love, Lord Mark Denham is here," which gave Margaret the sensation of having been mentally rubbed the wrong way, and made her feel that, in spite of her regard for Lord Mark, his visit would be very hateful to her. Her irritation evapor-

ated when she entered the sunshiny presence,
and listened to the genial talk; but returned
again and again throughout the evening.
For she could not divest herself of the con-
sciousness that her mother's eyes were following all her movements, with an expression
of mingled triumph and anxiety. And every
word that Mrs. Willoughby spoke seemed
to her like the bubbling of a concoction of
fear and exultation that was simmering
within the maternal mind.

But try as she would, she could not visit
her ill-humour on the kind friend who was so
gentle in his manner towards her. He found
her unaffectedly gracious, naïve, and sweet,
as usual, and his sanguine mind almost
fancied, now and again, that it detected an
added softness in her looks and tones. So
that the hopes which her mild rebuffs had
kept at bay for so long, were now determined
to have their way, and obtain, without farther
delay, their doom of either life or death. He
had come in obedience to frequent reminders
that he would be always welcome, had
modestly made as though he were " passing

that way, and had looked in for half an hour,"
but had accepted the invitation to remain
the night without much urging. And his
doubtful reply to Mrs. Willoughby's hope
that his visit would be prolonged for as much
time as he could spare was followed by a
glance at Margaret, which was not lost upon
her mother.

The evening was agreeable. But when, at
its close, Margaret went up to her room, all
her peace of mind and all her mirth had
vanished far away. For at a sudden touch,
at the careless mention of a name, of an
accidental, unimportant meeting, longings
which had before been resting in quiet
slumber had instantaneously been recalled to
wakefulness, life, and activity ! In the last
few minutes of standing up talk,—the lingering words on a favourite artist, and a picture
in the Royal Academy Exhibition of the
season,—Lord Mark Denham had mentioned
a meeting with an old acquaintance of his,
" Charles Meredith, a connoisseur in pictures," and had spoken of a striking observation made by him, and his wisht hat a certain

discussion could have been continued, adding, "But that restless being, Meredith,
was obliged to be off to some scientific
meeting, and was flying out of town, and
over the world, on wings of lightning, as
usual!"

With her head half averted, and with a
smile that had hardly hidden a sudden look
of fatigue, Margaret had bidden Lord Mark
good-night, and followed Mrs. Willoughby
up to bed. And then, unavailing regrets,
dark thoughts, the feeling that all things
in the world were at cross purposes, and that
certain evil beings of contrariety were permitted to work their mischievous deeds according to their own will, came over her with
the force of past days. This year was the
first, for several years, on which she and her
mother had not gone up to town, for some
part of the season. It had been her own
desire not to go; but had they gone, had
they, as on other occasions, been Lord Mark
Denham's companions at the Royal Academy, who could say what might not have
happened? At least, she might have dis-

covered if he were happy and satisfied without her!

So poor Lord Mark had few of Margaret's thoughts that night, and Mrs. Willoughby's fabric of hopes was frail as it appeared fair and brilliant.

CHAPTER XVIII.

AT eleven o'clock the next morning the catastrophe took place. By one o'clock the guest had departed. And Margaret, sad, thoughtful, anxious, with pale and tear-stained cheeks, was seated near the drawing-room window, alone. Her chin rested in her hand, and she was very still; except that at any fancied sound in the passages, or on the stair-case, she turned her head for an instant, in fear lest the dreaded moment of her mother's coming down should be at hand. She was determined that, if possible, she would keep Lord Mark Denham's proposal, and her own rejection of him, a secret between herself and him. But it would take a little time to regain her composure, and to prepare herself to make his apologies in a sufficiently natural and nonchalant manner.

" There she is ! " she exclaimed, at length. And hastily rising from her chair, she hurried across the room to look at herself in the glass over the fire-place, rubbed her cheeks, swept away the last remnant of a tear, smiled, grinned, and finally turned a beaming face upon her mother, as she entered the room.

" Well, my love," said Mrs. Willoughby, languidly, but with a cheerful smile, " what have you been about this morning ? I am very sorry I was unable to be down sooner ; but I have no doubt you have got on very well without me. What have you done with Lord Mark ? I expected to find you out of doors, lionizing him over the grounds."

" Oh, he left all sorts of messages and apologies for you, mother dear," answered Margaret, speaking very quickly, whilst her cheeks became crimson; "but he was obliged to go this morning. He found he could not stay any longer."

Mrs. Willoughby looked aghast, and stood for a moment silent, as though petrified by horror and astonishment.

" Gone, Margaret! What do you mean ? Speak,—explain yourself! Is this all a foolish joke of yours? Speak, can't you, child? How can Lord Mark have gone, when he promised to stay,—when——"

"You know, mother, he spoke doubtfully; he was not sure that he should be able to remain," interrupted Margaret, quailing beneath her mother's withering glance, and, despite all her efforts, blushing more furiously than ever.

"Margaret, you cannot deceive me," answered her mother. "I see,—I understand now; he has proposed to you, and you have refused him! And yet,—no, it is impossible! You cannot have been such a cruel, heartless flirt! After all the encouragement you have given him, after your conduct last night! It is impossible, Margaret!—tell me that it is impossible!—tell me what it all means !

"It means, mother, darling," cried Margaret, finding herself driven into a corner,— "it means that I love you too dearly ever to leave you. It means that I want to stay

with you always, if you will only let me, and
to be a very happy old maid!"

"It means rather, Margaret," replied her
mother, in a slowly reproachful tone, "that
you are bent upon displeasing me in every
possible way, and care for nothing so that
you may gratify your own vanity and
pleasure! No matter to you how many
hearts you trample under your feet!"

"Mother!" exclaimed Margaret, her lips
curling contemptuously, in spite of herself,
while a struggle went on within her, to
repress either laughter or weeping, or both.
Her sense of the ludicrous was tickled,
but her mother's absurd exaggeration, mis-
apprehension, and injustice, at the same
time, pained her to the quick. "Mother,"
she continued, "Lord Mark understands me
better than you do. He does not consider
me a heartless flirt. He knows that I like him
very, very, much, but cannot love him as a
man ought to be loved by his wife! Oh,
mother dear, if you would only forgive me,
as he does!" And kneeling down, she
leaned her head upon her mother's lap,

longing to sob her heart out there, as she had done, oftentimes, when a little child. But Mrs. Willoughby did not respond to her caressing tone.

Margaret," she said, " this is all very well; but I wish you would remember that ' to obey is better than sacrifice,' that—" but before her mother could proceed farther, Margaret had jumped up to her feet again, and the rising tears were driven back to their fountain, while, with a gay laugh, she said,—

" But, dear mother, you know that I am not offering to make any sacrifice ! And you know that I am always ready to obey you in every *possible* way ! "

" You have shown your obedience strangely, Margaret," it seems to me," returned Mrs. Willoughby, in a freezing tone. " You have thwarted all my wishes,— you have disappointed all my hopes ! And when I venture to reprove you, in the gentlest tone, you only stand and laugh at me ! When you have driven your mother into her grave, perhaps you will be sorry for your undutiful conduct ! "

Poor Margaret! She knew by heart her mother's favourite suggestions about an early grave, and had been threatened with remorseful orphanage so many times that the threat might well-nigh have lost something of its effect. But despite the vanity and frequency of repetition, her heart and conscience regularly rose to the bait thrown out to them, and now, looking remorsefully into her mother's pale face and heavy aching eyes,

"Mother dear," she said, "forgive me, I did not mean to laugh. Indeed, I am very, very unhappy; but what can I do?"

"Try to conquer your spirit of contradiction, my love; it is all I ask. You have disappointed me about poor Miles,—and I am sure it goes to one's heart to see the mere shadow that the poor fellow has become!—You have disappointed me about Sir Thomas Fletcher,—and now, when I thought your happiness was sure, when I thought that you had found all that heart could desire, you have disappointed me again! So delightful, so attractive, so good, so genial!—so— Margaret, I thought that even you could find nothing to complain of in Lord Mark Denham, and I was prepared to overlook your want of appreciation of poor Miles Grantham, who, certainly, poor fellow, is not so charming or elegant as Lord Mark, —and now, as I say, you have cruelly, cruelly disappointed me once more. Surely it can only be a spirit of contradiction that actuates you! You confess you like him! Think better of it, Margaret. Tell me,— why will you not marry him?"

"If I liked and admired him less, if I thought him less noble and good, I should think it less utterly out of the question that I could be brought to agree to marry him!" answered Margaret, quickly.

"What an extraordinary girl you are!" answered her mother, peevishly. "Am I not right in calling you perverse? You won't marry Miles because you hate him, and you won't marry Lord Mark because you like him. This seems to be all the rhyme or reason that is to be got out of you!"

"I should not consider myself so entirely base if I married Miles, whom I hate, as I should if I married Lord Mark, whom I honour, but whom I cannot love as he deserves to be loved by his wife! Now, mother, do you understand what I mean?" said Margaret.

"It is not always the noblest and the best upon whom we bestow our affections! We often love the faulty man the better for all his many failings!" returned Mrs. Willoughby, bringing her somewhat irrelevant answer out of a hoard of book-sayings which she kept somewhere locked up in the corner of her memory. A sudden notion had entered her head,—a sudden hope. She remembered to have read some novel in which a girl was represented as having veiled her affection for her lover under hatred, or even to have made herself believe that she hated the man whom, in heart, she loved with deep affection. Could this be the state of the case with Margaret's feelings for Miles? Could Lord Mark's proposal have revealed to her the fact that she really

loved Miles, and could marry no one else?
It must be so! Yes, the more she thought
of it, the more convinced she felt that so
it must be! And if a doubt crossed her
mind, it was quickly crushed, for that so it
should be she was firmly resolved. If Margaret had not the taste to return the love
of the fascinating young noblemen and
baronets who lost their hearts to her, and
danced attendance upon her season after
season in London, she should marry her
pretended pet aversion, the excellent young
man who had been devoted to her all her
life, and who, after all, was as eligible as
any of her more brilliant admirers. It would
be much more homelike, much less trouble;
it had been her first wish, and should be
her last. The Hall and The Cottage being
so close, everything being so comfortable
and luxurious, made the plan a very pleasant
one to fall back upon. And Mrs. Willoughby felt sure that it must have been ordered
especially, in consideration of her own
delicate health. But she was determined
to keep her thoughts to herself, and Mar-

garet could not make her out at all, that
day. She had become so preternaturally
amiable all of a sudden, and was so restless
and flighty in her manner, one minute, and
so dully and languidly reflective the next,
that her daughter remembered with horror
the caution that Mr. Thomas had given her
years before, and began almost to fear that
disappointment and worry were seriously
affecting her mother's mind. She reproached
herself remorsefully with doing nothing to
please her, and set about trying to soothe
and console her in every possible way she
could think of. When, with a sidelong
glance at Margaret, Mrs. Willoughby wondered how the Granthams were getting on,
when they were coming back, and whether
Miles would keep to his intention of going
North for the 12th of August, or would find
himself irresistibly drawn southwards, Margaret entered into her humour, sympathised
with her wonderings, and hoped that she
would not be much longer without the companionship of Lady Grantham. In the
evening, though she complained that her

head ached furiously, Mrs. Willoughby was animated and excited. At night Margaret was continually awakened by moans, and mutterings, and soliloquy; and presently she awoke with a start, to find the room lighted, and Mrs. Willoughby in the act of seating herself to her writing-table, with pen, ink, and paper, in readiness for correspondence.

"Mother dear, what is the matter?" cried Margaret, in great horror; "what are you up for at this time of night? Is it anything that I can do for you? Do get into bed again, or you'll be half dead all to-morrow."

"My dear," returned her mother, in a reassuring tone of voice, "go to sleep and leave me alone. I can't rest myself for thinking of poor Lord Mark's grief, and every thought brings a fresh throb of agony to my poor head. So I am trying to distract my mind by writing one of the many letters that my poor health has prevented my writing sooner. I owe dear Lady Grantham a letter, and she will be interested in hearing our news."

" All right, mother, only don't be long, there's a darling."

But Mrs. Willoughby was very long. In a lengthy and roundabout way she gave her reasons for believing that Margaret was not so indifferent to Miles as had hitherto been supposed, and hinted that it would be well for him not to put off too long returning to the assault of the sensitive child's heart !'

And amidst uncomfortable sleepings and wakings, Margaret heard the continuous scritch-scratch of her mother's pen until dawn, when she lay down again, to remain a useless being through the hours of daylight.

CHAPTER XIX.

MARGARET's predictions had been fulfilled.
Mrs. Willoughby was much the worse for
her midnight exertions, and during that day,
aud many other days, she caused her daughter
great anxiety. Agitations of various sorts
had their own way with her weak mind and
uncontrolled nervous system ; and more than
once Jane, the maid, frightened poor Margaret
nearly out of her wits by coming in with a
gloomy face and an alarming manner, to say,—

"Missis seems quite 'hoff her head' again,
Miss Margaret; I don't think we shall keep
her here much longer, if she goes on having
so many things to worry her. She'll be
going out like the snuff of a candle, Miss
Margaret, before you know where you are,
and them as has worried her won't be able to
bring her back again."

"Do you think she is going to have one of those horrid attacks of fever, Jane?" asked Margaret. "I wish Mr. Thomas was at home. We must send for some one."

"There, no doctors can save missis from being worried into her grave, and she is set against seeing the strange doctor, who acted so cruel to her the day he came in to see cook, and she spoke to him, with her poor eyes half shut with pain. She won't see him, so it ain't no use your troubling yourself to send for him, Miss Margaret."

Jane was right. Mrs. Willoughby refused, absolutely, to see Mr. Thomas' substitute when he came. She had taken an aversion from him, and declared that he was a man of no sympathy, and could not understand her peculiar constitution and sensitive temperament. No one could, she thought, now that he was away, but that usually much-abused and long-suffering person, Mr. Thomas! In short, Mrs. Willoughby seemed to be bent, at present, on martyrising herself. Margaret could do nothing with her, and was getting quite into despair, when relief came in the

shape of a letter from Lady Grantham,
with the intelligence that she and Sir John
were about to return to Grantham immedi-
ately, and she thought it more than probable
that their nephew Miles would accompany
them. It mattered little to Margaret, now,
whether he came or not. The nuisance of
his presence would not hurt her, and she
hailed gladly the prospect of any diversion
which might act as a remedy for Mrs. Willoughby's diseased state of nerves.

"Oh, Lady Grantham, I am so glad to see
you!" cried Margaret, when Lady Grantham appeared at The Cottage, on the morning after her arrival at home. "Mamma is
dreadfully ill. She has been hysterical
nearly all the morning, but it will do her
good to see you."

"I will go up to her, my dear. I'll find
the way. Don't come with me," replied
Lady Grantham, first with an air of concern,
and then with the most beaming of meaning
smiles. "Dear Miles is just outside the
door," she added. "I could not make him
come in, he was afraid of intruding. You

know what a shy and sensitive creature he is,
my darling! You can do what you like
about him, but I said I would tell you."

"All right, Lady Grantham," returned
Margaret, without responding to her friend's
cheerful manner, while, to herself, she sighed
out her favourite and oft-repeated pun, "Oh,
that he were miles away!"

"May I come in, Margaret?" called a
plaintive voice from the hall-door.

"By all means," replied Margaret, with
cold civility. "How do you do, Miles?"

He had been almost prepared for her
throwing herself into his arms, and felt
somewhat rebuffed by her chilly manner
and mere touch of the hand.

"Shy, perhaps, or hurt with me,—thinks
I am making up to others," he reflected, re-
assuringly, adding aloud, "It seems very
long since I saw you, dear Margaret."

Margaret's only response was a look of
amazement at his daring to use a term of
endearment towards her.

"May I not hope that the time has also
seemed the least bit long to you, Mar-

garet?" he went on, with a timid glance from under his eyelids.

"So long that,—forgive me, but I almost forget when last we met," she replied, with a laugh.

"'Forget!' Oh, Margaret, I thought,—I hoped,— Margaret, are you angry with me still?"

"Angry? Angry—what about?" replied Margaret, brusquely. "Please, we don't want any more nonsense to-day, Miles." Then, altering her tone to one of common-place unconcern, "I had no idea," she said, "that you were thinking of coming down here this August. I fancied that you were on your way to Scotland for the twelfth?"

"I—I—I heard something that made me change my mind. I hoped—I thought— Oh don't tell me that my hopes are to be disappointed again! It would kill me, Margaret! it would kill me! Oh, Margaret, have you been deceiving us all again? Was it not true what I heard?—that—that—that you were learning to love me a little?—that—that I might hope at last——"

Sheer astonishment had kept Margaret dumb while he spoke, but as he approached her, and, kneeling down, prepared to take her hand, and raise it to his lips, in what he conceived to be the most approved fashion, she jumped up from her chair, and, drawing quickly back from him, said,——

"What you mean by all this I have not the slightest conception, Miles. It appears to me that you are labouring under some sort of extraordinary hallucination, and the sooner you free yourself from it the better. I assure you your hopes, as you are pleased to express yourself, are entirely deceptive!"

"Then my aunt and all the rest have lied to me," said Miles, suddenly throwing off all softness of manner, rising hastily from the lowly position which he had assumed, and striding towards the door. "And you, Margaret, *you*—" He left her to complete the sentence for herself, and was off like a shot.

A sense of the ludicrous, for the moment, overcame all else in Margaret's mind, and her excitement found relief in an uncontrollable fit of laughter.

In this state she was found by Lady
Grantham, who had hastened down to learn
the meaning of the banging of the front
door, which had brought forth a complaining "Oh!" from Mrs. Willoughby, and
had occasioned all manner of painful con-
tortions of her face.

The sight of Lady Grantham sobered
Margaret in a moment. "Is anything the
matter?" she asked, quickly. Is mamma—"

"I find your mother exceedingly changed,
Margaret," replied Lady Grantham, severely.
"I think her much worse, and I do not
wonder at it. She has had to go through a
great deal, poor dear. I have come down
for her, to see what the noise was?"

"Noise? Was there a noise, Lady Grantham?"

"Who slammed the door in that thought-
less manner?" returned Lady Grantham."
"Is Miles gone already? I thought you would
have had much to say to each other."

"Well,—no,—not very much. That is to
say, he went off in a great hurry, and I am
afraid he must, in his haste, have been guilty

of slamming the door. I wish he had not, because of poor mamma's head."

"Why did he go away in such a hurry?" asked Lady Grantham, fixing her eyes on Margaret, in a manner that seemed to say, "I am not going to let you off, so you need not think it." "It is all very well for you to pretend that nothing of importance has happened. You know better, and I know better. Margaret, you are killing your mother! I am quite shocked at the change I find in her."

"I will go to mamma," said Margaret, sadly. "Please excuse me, Lady Grantham."

"I promised to return to her, replied Lady Grantham, hastily, passing Margaret, and moving towards the stair-case. "She is waiting to know the result of Miles' interview with you, and if it is disappointing, I will soothe her to the best of my power. Tell me, Margaret——"

"Interview!" interrupted Margaret, in a tone of amazed impatience. "Interview! Did she know that he was coming? Did she expect anything? Please explain what it all means, Lady Grantham?"

" I think it is you whose conduct needs explanation, my dear," said Lady Grantham. " You gave your mamma to understand that you had discovered your mistake, that you had found out the worth of Miles' heart at last."

" My dear Lady Grantham, you must be dreaming ! " cried Margaret, her tone betraying an almost equal amount of astonishment and dismay. " What could I have said that mamma could so have misunderstood ! "

" The wonder would be if the moods of so capricious a young lady were always comprehended, my dear, rather than that they should be continually misunderstood," returned Lady Grantham, in a displeased tone of voice. " But so long as you have your own way, Margaret, I believe you care little what misery you cause to others ! "

Margaret knew that the words were unjust, and yet they struck home to her heart, and gave it a sharp pang, and while her companion proceeded to Mrs. Willoughby's room, she remained pondering over them, at the bottom of the stair-case.

"After all," she said to herself,—"after all, perhaps she may be right. For whom do I live? Who but I myself would suffer if I were to sacrifice myself, and do what she wants? Would *he* care? Have I any right to suppose that, after all these years, he still thinks of me? And if he does not, is it not mere sentimental selfish nonsense my going on dreaming of that happy and sorrowful long-past time? If I cannot make any one else happy, by things coming right, why may I not as well make myself unhappy to please mamma? It will be doing something. It will bring all this worry to an end, and we should have peace for a little while: I should of course be miserable, but what does that signify? What would be better than misery for mamma's sake? But would it be wicked, as I hate him so?"

She was so in love with the notion of self-sacrifice that she did not stay to receive an answer to her mental query, but quickly went on with her silent parley,—

"It would be to save mamma, and though I could never learn to like him, I would make him a dutiful wife for her sake. And if she gets well and is happy, will it not be worth while for me to be miserable?"

With her heart and mind thus full of thought and feeling, she went into her mother's room, where she found Mrs. Willoughby in violent hysterics, Lady Grantham bending soothingly over her, and Jane standing at the bottom of the bed, looking on hopelessly, with the knowledge that a dash of cold water would be more to the purpose than sympathising words.

"Oh, that Mr. Thomas were here! For he knows how to soothe mamma's nerves without kneeling down to worship them, like the rest of the world!" thought Margaret, whose self-sacrificing resolve seemed suddenly to have revealed to her something of the weakness and selfishness of her mother's character; and who, with the sense of all that she was intending to give up for her mother's sake, felt doubly irritated by the scene upon which she had entered.

"Jane, you need not stay," she said to the lady's-maid, and there was something in Margaret's manner that seemed to enforce obedience.   Then, armed with *eau-de-cologne* and cold water, she took up her station at the side of the bed, opposite to that at which Lady Grantham stood, and firmly, though gently, proceeded to conquer the attack.   But though the cure had been effected, Mrs. Willoughby shrank away from her daughter, and with feeble moans, which, in spite of herself, made Margaret very cross, put out her hands to Lady Grantham, and looked imploringly towards her.

"I won't leave you, my dear," said her sympathising friend, softly, while she shot forth a reproachful glance at Margaret.

"Mother, dear, don't you think you had better try to go to sleep now?" said Margaret, laying her hand softly on Mrs. Willoughby's forehead.   And it seemed as if, she had suddenly gained some strange ascendancy over others.   Mrs. Willoughby ceased her moaning, and closed her eyes, and composed her face, and Lady Grantham, seeing there was no longer any part for her to perform, with a cold farewell to Margaret, took her leave; and remembering a like scene

of years ago, it seemed to Margaret as if a
bad dream had come to life in reality.

But her feelings were very different, as she
now sat and ruminated, while her mother
slept, from what they had been in that same
room seven years before. Then a fair dream-
land had cast its spells around her. Now she
was bidding farewell to happy dreams, and
strengthening her self-sacrificing resolution,
and only arranging her plans so as to leave
herself a faint loop-hole of hope for the future.

"Mother," she said, presently, when her
mother awakened from her doze, "I want to
say something to you. Is your head well
enough to bear talking?"

"Margaret!" cried Mrs. Willoughby,
sitting up, and speaking in a querulous tone,
which grew louder and shriller as she went
on,—"Margaret, your cruel, undutiful conduct is killing me. I don't want to hear
any more about it. Let me die in peace;
you won't have me to disturb you much
longer!" Then lying down with a martyr-
like expression of countenance, she languidly closed her eyes.

"Mother," said Margaret, "do you still wish that I should marry Miles Grantham?"

Mrs. Willoughby opened her eyes and looked up briskly.

"You know my wishes, Margaret," she replied. "Why do you ask? Are you going to deceive me with false promises again?"

"Have I deceived you mother?" said Margaret, quietly,—"well, I will not deceive you again. Listen, mother! If, in spite of all that I have said, he still wishes it, and if you and his people wish it, I will consent to marry Miles on condition that he keeps away from me for a twelvemonth, and that if anything should occur during that time to alter your mind and mine, or to change his feelings towards me, the engagement shall be considered at an end."

"My child, my darling!" exclaimed Mrs. Willoughby, rapturously. "I knew it,—I knew it! I was sure that in your heart you loved him! You——"

"But I don't love him, mother," put in Margaret. "If I marry him, it will be solely to please you."

" You will never regret it ! You will be happy ! He will have the best of wives ! We shall all be happy ! You little know how thankful and glad you have made me, my child."

This was delightful ! For a moment, Margaret almost forgot everything else in the pleasure of being caressed and petted by her mother, whom she loved as fondly as if she had been the wisest and most unselfish of women.

" Now, mother dear," she said, presently, I shall leave you to rest."

" No, I am quite rested ; I am ready to get up," answered Mrs. Willoughby.

How delightful, to be able to charm away pain and languor by humouring an invalid's wishes, and letting her have her own way ! Margaret found her immediate reward to be exceedingly satisfactory.

Early in the afternoon Mrs. Willoughby and Lady Grantham held another private conference ; which was followed by another " lovers' interview," to use Lady Grantham's expression ; and in the evening a friendly meeting took place at The Cottage, for re-joicing over the happy arrangement that had been entered into. It was the merriest evening possible, and Margaret herself was the merriest of the party. Who, to look at her radiant face, and listen to her joyous laugh, could have doubted that she was happy? Even she herself, in her excitement, began to think that the charms of martyrdom surpassed all other charms to be experienced on earth!

END OF VOL. I.

SAMUEL TINSLEY'S

PUBLICATIONS.

London:

SAMUEL TINSLEY,

10, SOUTHAMPTON STREET, STRAND.

. *Totally distinct from any other firm of Publishers.*

NOTICE.

The *PRINTING* and *PUBLICATION* of all Classes of *BOOKS*, *Pamphlets*, &c.— *Apply to* Mr. Samuel Tinsley, *Publisher*, 10, *Southampton Street*, *Strand*, *London*, *W.C.*

SAMUEL TINSLEY'S
NEW PUBLICATIONS.

THE POPULAR NEW NOVELS, AT ALL LIBRARIES IN TOWN
AND COUNTRY.

A DESPERATE CHARACTER: a Tale of the Gold
Fever. By W. THOMSON-GREGG. 3 vols., 31s. 6d.

"A novel which cannot fail to interest."—*Daily News.*

A LDEN OF ALDENHOLME. By GEORGE SMITH.
3 vols., 31s. 6d.

"Pure and graceful. . . . . Above the average."—*Athenæum.*

A LICE GODOLPHIN and A LITTLE HEIRESS.
By MARY NEVILLE. In 2 vols. 21s.

A NNALS of the TWENTY-NINTH CENTURY;
or, the Autobiography of the Tenth President of the
World-Republic. 3 vols., 31s. 6d.

"From beginning to end the book is one long catalogue of wonders. . . .
Very amusing, and will doubtless create some little sensation."—*Scotsman.*
"By mere force of originality will more than hold its own among the
rank and file of fiction."—*Examiner.*
"Here is a work in certain respects one of the most singular in modern
literature, which surpasses all of its class in bold and luxuriant imagination,
in vivid descriptive power, in startling—not to say extravagant suggestions
—in lofty and delicate moral sympathies. It is difficult to read it with a
serious countenance: yet it is impossible not to read it with curious interest,
and sometimes with profound admiration. The author's imagination hath
run mad, but often there is more in his philosophy than the world may
dream of. . . . . We have read his work with almost equal feelings of
pleasure, wonderment, and amusement, and this, we think, will be the
feelings of most of its readers. On the whole, it is a book of remarkable
novelty and unquestionable genius."—*Nonconformist.*

A S THE FATES WOULD HAVE IT. By G.
BERESFORD FITZGERALD. Crown 8vo., 10s. 6d.

Samuel Tinsley, 10, Southampton Street, Strand.

A WOMAN TO BE WON. An Anglo-Indian Sketch. By ATHENE BRAMA. 2 vols., 21s.

> " She is a woman, therefore may be wooed ;
> She is a woman, therefore may be won."
>   —TITUS ANDRONICUS, Act ii., Sc. I.

" A welcome addition to the literature connected with the most picturesque of our dependencies."—*Athenæum.*

" As a tale of adventure " A Woman to be Won " is entitled to decided commendation."—*Graphic.*

" A more familiar sketch of station life in India . . . . has never been written. . . . ."—*Nonconformist.*

" . . . . Very well told."—*Public Opinion.*

BARBARA'S WARNING. By the Author of " Recommended to Mercy." 3 vols., 31s. 6d.

BETWEEN TWO LOVES. By ROBERT J. GRIFFITHS, LL.D. 3 vols., 31s. 6d.

BLUEBELL. By Mrs. G. C. HUDDLESTON. 3 vols., 31s. 6d.

BORN TO BE A LADY. By KATHERINE HENDERSON. Crown 8vo., 7s. 6d.

" Miss Henderson has written a really interesting story. . . . The heroine, Jeanie Monroe, is just what a Jeanie should be—'bonny,' 'sonsie,' 'douce,' and 'eident,'—having a fair and sound mind in a fair and sound body ; loving and loyal, true to earthly love, and firm to heavenly faith. The novelist's art is exhibited by marrying this gardener's daughter to a man of shifting principles, higher in a sense than she in the social scale. . . . The 'local colouring' is excellent, and the subordinate characters, Jeanie's father especially, capital studies."—*Athenæum.*

BUILDING UPON SAND. By ELIZABETH J. LYSAGHT. Crown 8vo., 10s. 6d.

" It is an eminently lady-like story, and pleasantly told. . . . . We can safely recommend 'Building upon Sand.'"—*Graphic.*

CHASTE AS ICE, PURE AS SNOW. By Mrs. M. C. DESPARD. 3 vols., 31s. 6d. Second Edition.

" A novel of something more than ordinary promise."—*Graphic.*

CLAUDE HAMBRO. By JOHN C. WESTWOOD. 3 vols., 31s. 6d.

CRUEL CONSTANCY. By KATHARINE KING, Author of 'The Queen of the Regiment.' 3 vols., 31s. 6d.

" It is a very readable novel, and contains much pleasant writing."—*Pall Mall Gazette.*

DISINTERRED. From the Boke of a Monk of Carden Abbey. By T. ESMONDE. Crown 8vo., 7s. 6d.

DR. MIDDLETON'S DAUGHTER. By the Author of " A Desperate Character." 3 vols., 31s. 6d.

DULCIE. By LOIS LUDLOW. 3 vols., 31s. 6d.

FAIR, BUT NOT FALSE. By EVELYN CAMPBELL. 3 vols., 31s. 6d.

FAIR, BUT NOT WISE. By Mrs. FORREST-GRANT. 2 vols., 21s.

" ' Fair but not Wise' possesses considerable merit, and is both cleverly and powerfully written. If earnest, it is yet amusing and sometimes humorous, and the interest is well sustained from the first to the last page."—*Court Express.*

FIRST AND LAST. By F. VERNON-WHITE. 2 vols., 21s.

FLORENCE; or, Loyal Quand Même. By FRANCES ARMSTRONG. Crown 8vo., 5s., cloth. Post free.

"A very charming love story, eminently pure and lady-like in tone, effective and interesting in plot, and, rarest praise of all, written in excellent English."—*Civil Service Review.*

" The book is excellently printed and nicely bound—in fact it is one which authoress, publisher, and reader may alike regard with mingled satisfaction and pleasure."—*Nottingham Daily Guardian.*

FAIR IN THE FEARLESS OLD FASHION. By CHARLES FARMLET. 2 vols., 21s.

FOLLATON PRIORY. 2 vols., 21s.

FRIEDEMANN BACH; or, The Fortunes of an Idealist. (Adapted from the German of A. E. BRACHVOGEL.) Dedicated, with permission, to H.R.H. the PRINCESS CHRISTIAN of SCHLESWIG-HOLSTEIN. 1 vol., crown 8vo, 7s. 6d.

GAUNT ABBEY. By ELIZABETH J. LYSAGHT, Author of " Building upon Sand," " Nearer and Dearer," etc. 3 vols., 31s. 6d.

GOLDEN MEMORIES. By EFFIE LEIGH. 2 vols., 21s.

" There is not a dull page in the book."—*Morning Post.*

GRAYWORTH: a Story of Country Life. By CAREY HAZELWOOD. 3 vols., 31s. 6d.

GRANTHAM SECRETS. By PHŒBE M. FEILDEN. 3 vols. 31s. 6d.

GREED'S LABOUR LOST. By the Author of "Recommended to Mercy," etc. 3 vols., 31s. 6d.

HER GOOD NAME. By J. FORTREY BOUVERIE. 3 vols., 31s. 6d.

"Abundance of stirring incident . . . and plenty of pathos and fun justify it in taking a place among the foremost novels of the day."—*Morning Post.*

"Amusing descriptions of hunting scenes."—*Athenæum.*

"A clever novel."—*Scotsman.*

"The interest is sustained from first to last."—*Irish Times.*

"A really interesting novel."—*Dublin Evening Mail.*

"Displays a good deal of cleverness.   There is real . . . humour in some of the scenes. The author has drawn one sweet and womanly character, that of the ill-used heroine."—*Spectator.*

"To an interesting and well-constructed plot we have added vigorous writing and sketches of character. . . . . Altogether, the novel is one that will justify the re-appearance of its author in the same character at an early date."—*Field.*

HER IDOL. By MAXWELL HOOD. 3 vols., 31s. 6d.

HILDA AND I. By MRS. WINCHCOMBE HARTLEY. 2 vols., 21s.

"An interesting, well-written, and natural story."—*Public Opinion.*

"For a novel of good tone, lively plot, and singular absence of vulgarity, we can honestly commend 'Hilda and I.'"—*English Churchman.*

HILLESDEN ON THE MOORS. By ROSA MAC-KENZIE KETTLE, Author of "The Mistress of Langdale Hall." 2 vols., 21s.

"Thoroughly enjoyable, full of pleasant thoughts gracefully expressed, and eminently pure in tone."—*Public Opinion.*

IN BONDS, BUT FETTERLESS: a Tale of Old Ulster. By RICHARD CUNINGHAM. 2 vols., 21s.

IN SECRET PLACES. By ROBERT J. GRIFFITHS, LL.D. 3 vols., 31s. 6d.

IS IT FOR EVER? By KATE MAINWARING. 3 vols., 31s. 6d.

"A work to be recommended. . . . . A thrillingly sensational novel."—*Sunday Times.*

JOHN FENN'S WIFE. By MARIA LEWIS. Crown 8vo., 7s. 6d.

KATE BYRNE. By S. HOWARD TAYLOR. 2 vols., 21s.

KITTY'S RIVAL. By SYDNEY MOSTYN, Author of 'The Surgeon's Secret,' etc. 3 vols., 31s. 6d.

"Essentially dramatic and absorbing. . . . . We have nothing but unqualified praise for 'Kitty's Rival,' which we recommend as a fresh and natural story, full of homely pathos and kindly humour, and written in a style which shows the good sense of the author has been cultivated by the study of the works of the best of English writers."—*Public Opinion*.

LORD CASTLETON'S WARD. By Mrs. B. R. GREEN. 3 vols., 31s. 6d.

"There is a great deal of love-making in the book, an element which will no doubt favourably recommend it to the notice of young lady readers. . . . Being a novel suited to the popular taste, it is likely to become a favourite. . . . Sensationalism is evidently aimed at, and here the author has succeeded admirably. . . . Mrs. Green has written a novel which will hold the reader entranced from the first page to the last. . . . Emphatically a sensational novel of no ordinary merit, with plenty of stirring incident well and vividly worked out. . . . Florence de Malcé, the heroine and Lord Castleton's ward, is a masterpiece."—*Morning Post*.

MARRIED FOR MONEY. 1 vol., 10s. 6d.

MARY GRAINGER: A Story. By GEORGE LEIGH. 2 vols., 21s.

"A very remarkable, a wholly exceptional book. It is original from beginning to end; it is full of indubitable power; the characters, if they are such as we are not accustomed to meet with in ordinary novels, are nevertheless wonderfully real, and the reader is able to recognise the force and truth of the author's conceptions. The heroine is such a creation as would be looked for in vain in literature outside the pages of Balzac or George Sand—a noble but undeveloped character, of whom, nevertheless, we are inclined to believe that many a counterpart is to be found in real life."—*Scotsman*.

MR. VAUGHAN'S HEIR. By FRANK LEE BENEDICT, Author of "Miss Dorothy's Charge," etc. 3 vols., 31s. 6d.

NEARER AND DEARER. By ELIZABETH J. LYSAGHT, Author of "Building upon Sand." 3 vols., 31s. 6d.

NEGLECTED; a Story of Nursery Education Forty Years Ago. By Miss JULIA LUARD. Crown 8vo., 5s. cloth.

NO FATHERLAND. By MADAME VON OPPEN.
2 vols., 21s.

NORTONDALE CASTLE. 1 vol., 7s. 6d.

NOT TO BE BROKEN. By W. A. CHANDLER.
Crown 8vo., 10s. 6d.

ONLY SEA AND SKY. By ELIZABETH HINDLEY.
2 vols., 21s.

"This is a tranquil story, very well told. There are several neat touches of character in these two volumes, and a fair amount of humour."—*Public Opinion.*

"A really good and readable novel—we hope only the precursor of others from the same pen."—*Scotsman.*

"By no means without promise."—*Globe.*

"This, on the whole, is a fairly written story. Monsieur Jules is a worthy Frenchman whom all readers will admire."—*Evening Standard.*

"The author seems to know something of France and Germany."—*Athenæum.*

OVER THE FURZE. By ROSA M. KETTLE, Author of the "Mistress of Langdale Hall," etc. 3 vols., 31s. 6d.

PERCY LOCKHART. By F. W. BAXTER. 2 vols., 21s.

PUTTYPUT'S PROTÉGÉE; or, Road, Rail, and River. A Story in Three Books. By HENRY GEORGE CHURCHILL. Crown 8vo., (uniform with "The Mistress of Langdale Hall"), with 14 illustrations by WALLIS MACKAY. Post free, 4s. Second edition.

"It is a lengthened and diversified farce, full of screaming fun and comic delineation—a reflection of Dickens, Mrs. Malaprop, and Mr. Boucicault, and dealing with various descriptions of social life. We have read and laughed, pooh-poohed, and read again, ashamed of our interest, but our interest has been too strong for our shame. Readers may do worse than surrender themselves to its melo-dramatic enjoyment. From title-page to colophon, only Dominie Sampson's epithet can describe it—it is 'prodigious.'"—*British Quarterly Review.*

"It is impossible to read 'Puttyput's Protégée' without being reminded at every turn of the contemporary stage, and the impression it leaves on the mind is very similar to that produced by witnessing a whole evening's entertainment at one of our popular theatres."—*Echo.*

RAVENSDALE. By ROBERT THYNNE, Author of "Tom Delany." 3 vols., 31s. 6d.

"A well-told, natural, and wholesome story."—*Standard*.
"No one can deny merit to the writer."—*Saturday Review*.

RUPERT REDMOND: A Tale of England, Ireland, and America. By WALTER SIMS SOUTHWELL. 3 vols., 31s. 6d.

SELF-UNITED. By Mrs. HICKES BRYANT. 3 vols., 31s. 6d.

SHINGLEBOROUGH SOCIETY. 3 vols., 31s. 6d.

SKYWARD AND EARTHWARD: a Tale. By ARTHUR PENRICE. 1 vol., crown 8vo, 7s. 6d.

SPOILT LIVES. By Mrs. RAPER. 1 vol., 7s. 6d.

SOME OF OUR GIRLS. By Mrs. EILOART, Author of "The Curate's Discipline," "The Love that Lived," "Meg," etc., etc. 3 vols., 31s. 6d.

"A book that should be read. . . . Ably written books directed to this purpose deserve to meet with the success which Mrs. Eiloart's work will obtain."—*Athenæum*.
"Altogether the book is well worth perusing."—*John Bull*.

SONS OF DIVES. 2 vols., 21s.

"A well-principled and natural story."—*Athenæum*.

STRANDED, BUT NOT LOST. By DOROTHY BROMYARD. 3 vols., 31s. 6d.

SWEET IDOLATRY. By DAMON. 1 vol., 7s. 6d.

"Love is a sweet idolatry enslaving all the soul,—
A mighty spiritual force, warring with the dulness of matter,—
An angel-mind breathed into a mortal, though fallen, yet how beautiful !
All the devotion of the heart, in all its depth and grandeur."
—TUPPER.

THE ADVENTURES OF MICK CALLIGHIN, M.P. a Story of Home Rule ; and THE DE BURGHOS, a Romance. By W. R. ANCKETILL. In one Volume, with Illustrations. Price 7s. 6d.

THE BARONET'S CROSS.   By Mary Meeke,
Author of "Marion's Path through Shadow to Sunshine."
2 vols., 21s.

THE BRITISH SUBALTERN.   By an Ex-
Subaltern. 1 vol., 7s. 6d.

THE D'EYNCOURTS OF FAIRLEIGH.   By
Thomas Rowland Skemp. 3 vols., 31s. 6d.

"An exceedingly readable novel, full of various and sustained interest.
. . . . . The interest is well kept up all through."—*Daily Telegraph.*

THE HEIR OF REDDESMONT. 3 vols., 31s. 6d.

" Full of interest and life." – *Echo.*

THE INSIDIOUS THIEF: a Tale for Humble
Folks. By One of Themselves. Crown 8vo., 5s. Second
Edition.

THE LOVE THAT LIVED. By Mrs. Eiloart, Author
of "The Curate's Discipline," "Just a Woman," "Woman's
Wrong," &c. 3 vols., 31s. 6d.

"Three volumes which most people will prefer not to leave till they have
read the last page of the third volume."—*Pall Mall Gazette.*
"One of the most thoroughly wholesome novels we have read for some
ime." —*Scotsman.*

THE MAGIC OF LOVE. By Mrs. Forrest-Grant,
Author of " Fair, but not Wise." 3 vols., 31s. 6d.

"A very amusing novel."—*Scotsman.*

THE MISTRESS OF LANGDALE HALL: a
Romance of the West Riding. By Rosa Mackenzie
Kettle. Complete in one handsome volume, with Frontispiece
and Vignette by Percival Skelton. 4s., post free.

"The story is interesting and very pleasantly written, and for the sake
of both author and publisher we cordially wish it the reception it deserves."
—*Saturday Review.*

THE SECRET OF TWO HOUSES. By Fanny
Fisher. 2 vols., 21s.

"Thoroughly dramatic."– *Public Opinion.*
"The story is well told."—*Sunday Times.*

THE SEDGEBOROUGH WORLD. By A. Fare-
brother. 2 vols., 21s.

Samuel Tinsley, 10, Southampton Street, Strand.

THE SURGEON'S SECRET. By SYDNEY MOSTYN, Author of "Kitty's Rival," etc. Crown 8vo., 10s. 6d.

"A most exciting novel—the best on our list. It may be fairly recommended as a very extraordinary book."—*John Bull.*

"A stirring drama, with a number of closely connected scenes, in which there are not a few legitimately sensational situations. There are many spirited passages."—*Public Opinion.*

THE THORNTONS OF THORNBURY. By Mrs. HENRY LOWTHER CHERMSIDE. 3 vols., 31s. 6d.

THE TRUE STORY OF HUGH NOBLE'S FLIGHT. By the Authoress of "What Her Face Said." 10s. 6d.

"A pleasant story, with touches of exquisite pathos, well told by one who is master of an excellent and sprightly style."—*Standard.*

THE WIDOW UNMASKED; or, the Firebrand in the Family. By FLORA F. WYLDE. 3 vols., 31s. 6d.

TIMOTHY CRIPPLE; or, "Life's a Feast." By THOMAS AURIOL ROBINSON. 2 vols., 21s.

"This is a most amusing book, and the author deserves great credit for the novelty of his design, and the quaint humour with which it is worked out."—*Public Opinion.*

"For abundance of humour, variety of incident, and idiomatic vigour of expression, Mr. Robinson deserves, and will no doubt receive, great credit."—*Civil Service Review.*

TOO LIGHTLY BROKEN. 3 vols., 31s. 6d.

"A very pleasing story . . . . . very prettily told."—*Morning Post.*

TOM DELANY. By ROBERT THYNNE, Author of "Ravensdale." 3 vols., 31s. 6d.

"A very bright, healthy, simply-told story."—*Standard.*

"All the individuals whom the reader meets at the gold-fields are well-drawn, amongst whom not the least interesting is 'Terrible Mac.'"—*Hour.*

"There is not a dull page in the book."—*Scotsman.*

TOWER HALLOWDEANE. 2 vols., 21s.

TOXIE: a Tale. 3 vols., 31s. 6d.

TWIXT CUP and LIP. By MARY LOVETT-CAMERON. 3 vols., 31s. 6d.

"Displays signs of more than ordinary promise. . . . As a whole the novel cannot fail to please. Its plot is one that will arrest attention; and its characters, one and all, are full of life and have that nameless charm which at once attracts and retains the sympathy of the reader."—*Daily News.*

'TWIXT WIFE AND FATHERLAND. 2 vols., 21s.

"A bright, vigorous, and healthy story, and decidedly above the average of books of this class. Being in two volumes it commands the reader's unbroken attention to the very end."—*Standard.*

"It is by someone who has caught her (Baroness Tautphoeus') gift of telling a charming story in the boldest manner, and of forcing us to take an interest in her characters, which writers, far better from a literary point of view, can never approach."—*Athenæum.*

"The story of Camilla's trials exhibits an unusual power of delineating not what is on the surface, but what is exercising the soul under a calm outward exterior."—*John Bull.*

"The tale has both freshness and power. The Italian conspirators are well sketched and individualised, and there are some delicious descriptions of Dolomite scenery which will incline many readers in that direction."—*Nonconformist.*

"There is originality in this story. . . . . Camilla had been foolish and headstrong, but she is rather a fascinating heroine."—*Graphic.*

"The description of Tyrolese life, and all the intrigues of De Zanna and his friends, with the counter-movements of the Austrian party, are not without interest."—*Morning Post.*

"The story is written in a quaint and easy style that is very refreshing ; and there are many enjoyable descriptive passages."—*Scotsman.*

"Shadows forth much promise. The story will be read with pleasure for the freshness of its descriptions of the people and glorious scenes of the South Tyrol."—*Morning Advertiser.*

TWO STRIDES OF DESTINY. By S. Brookes Bucklee. 3 vols., 31s. 6d.

"For an early effort the work is eminently satisfactory. It is quite original, the tone is good, the language graceful, and the characters thoroughly natural."—*Public Opinion.*

"A pretty story, written strictly in accordance with the popular taste in fiction. It is a thoughtful story. . . . Possesses many elements of originality."—*Morning Post.*

UNDER PRESSURE. By T. E. Pemberton. 2 vols., 21s.

"A novel above the average standard. . . . We will not detail the dramatic end of this interesting and well-written story."—*Daily News.*

"There is humour, character, and much clever description in 'Under Pressure,' and it is sure to be read with interest."—*Yorkshire Post.*

"Mr. Pemberton has displayed keen observation and high literary capacity."—*Birmingham Morning News.*

"One of the best contributions to light literature that has been published for some time."—*Birmingham Daily Gazette.*

"The book has very considerable vigour and originality."—*Scotsman.*

Samuel Tinsley, 10, Southampton Street, Strand.

WAGES: a Story in Three Books. 3 vols., 31s. 6d.

"A work of no commonplace character."—*Sunday Times.*

WANDERING FIRES. By Mrs. M. C. DESPARD, Author of "Chaste as Ice," &c. 3 vols., 31s. 6d.

WEBS OF LOVE. (I. A Lawyer's Device. II. Sancta Simplicitas.) By G. E. H. 1 vol., Crown 8vo., 10s. 6d.

WEIMAR'S TRUST. By Mrs. EDWARD CHRISTIAN. 3 vols., 31s. 6d.

"A novel which deserves to be read, and which, once begun, will not be readily laid aside till the end."—*Scotsman.*

WILL SHE BEAR IT? A Tale of the Weald. 3 vols., 31s. 6d.

"This is a clever story, easily and naturally told, and the reader's interest sustained throughout. . . . A pleasant, readable book, such as we can heartily recommend as likely to do good service in the dull and foggy days before us."—*Spectator.*

WOMAN'S AMBITION. By M. L. LYONS. 1 vol., 7s. 6d.

HOW I SPENT MY TWO YEARS' LEAVE; or, My Impressions of the Mother Country, the Continent of Europe, the United States of America, and Canada. By an Indian Officer. In one vol. 8vo. Handsomely bound. Price 15s.

FACT AGAINST FICTION. The Habits and Treatment of Animals Practically Considered. Hydrophobia and Distemper. With some remarks on Darwin. By the HON. GRANTLEY F. BERKELEY. 2 vols., 8vo., 30s.

MALTA SIXTY YEARS AGO. With a Concise History of the Order of St. John of Jerusalem, the Crusades, and Knights Templars. By Col. CLAUDIUS SHAW. Handsomely bound in cloth, 10s. 6d., gilt edges, 12s.

Samuel Tinsley, 10, Southampton Street, Strand.

HARRY'S BIG BOOTS: a Fairy Tale, for "Smalle Folke." By S. E. GAY. With 8 Full-page Illustrations and a Vignette by the author, drawn on wood by PERCIVAL SKELTON. Crown 8vo., handsomely bound in cloth, price 5s.

"Some capital fun will be found in 'Harry's Big Boots.'... The illustrations are excellent, and so is the story."—*Pall Mall Gazette.*

MOVING EARS. By the Ven. Archdeacon WEAKHEAD, Rector of Newtown, Kent. 1 vol., crown 8vo., 5s.

A TRUE FLEMISH STORY. By the Author of "The Eve of St. Nicholas." In wrapper, 1s.

THE PHYSIOLOGY OF THE SECTS. Crown 8vo., price 5s.

ANOTHER WORLD; or, Fragments from the Star City of Montalluyah. By HERMES. Third Edition, revised, with additions. Post 8vo., price 12s.

THE FALL OF MAN: An Answer to Mr. Darwin's "Descent of Man;" being a Complete Refutation, by common-sense arguments, of the Theory of Natural Selection. 1s., sewed.

THE RITUALIST'S PROGRESS; or, A Sketch of the Reforms and Ministrations of the Rev. Septimius Alban, Member of the E.C.U., Vicar of S. Alicia, Sloperton. By A. B. WILDERED, Parishioner. Fcp. 8vo. 2s. 6d. cloth.

MISTRESSES AND MAIDS. By HUBERT CURTIS, Author of "Helen," etc. Price 1d.

EPITAPHIANA; or, the Curiosities of Churchyard Literature: being a Miscellaneous Collection of Epitaphs, with an INTRODUCTION. By W. FAIRLEY. Crown 8vo., cloth, price 5s. Post free.

"Entertaining."—*Pall Mall Gazette.*
"A capital collection."—*Court Circular*
"A very readable volume."—*Daily Review.*
"A most interesting book."—*Leeds Mercury.*
"Interesting and amusing." *Nonconformist.*
"Particularly entertaining."—*Public Opinion.*
"A curious and entertaining volume."—*Oxford Chronicle.*
"A very interesting collection."—*Civil Service Gazette.*

TWELVE NATIONAL BALLADS (First Series). Dedicated to Liberals of all classes. By PHILHELOT, of Cambridge; in ornamental cover, price sixpence, post free.

POETRY, ETC.

THE DEATH OF ÆGEUS, and other Poems. By W. H. A. EMRA. Fcp. 8vo., 5s.

HELEN, and other Poems. By HUBERT CURTIS. Fcp. 8vo., 3s. 6d.

MISPLACED LOVE. A Tale of Love, Sin, Sorrow, and Remorse. 1 vol., crown 8vo., 5s.

THE SOUL SPEAKS, and other Poems. By FRANCIS H. HEMERY. In wrapper, 1s.

SUMMER SHADE AND WINTER SUNSHINE: Poems. By ROSA MACKENZIE KETTLE, Author of "The Mistress of Langdale Hall." New Edition. 2s. 6d., cloth.

THE WITCH of NEMI, and other Poems. By EDWARD BRENNAN. Crown 8vo., 10s. 6d.

MARY DESMOND, AND OTHER POEMS. By NICHOLAS J. GANNON. Fcp. 8vo., 4s., cloth. Second Edition.

THE GOLDEN PATH: a Poem. By ISABELLA STUART. 6d., sewed.

THE REDBREAST OF CANTERBURY CATHE-DRAL: Lines from the Latin of Peter du Moulin, some-time a Prebendary of Canterbury. Translated by the Rev. F. B. WELLS, M.A., Rector of Woodchurch. Handsomely bound, price 1s.

THE TICHBORNE AND ORTON AUTOGRAPHS comprising Autograph Letters of Roger Tichborne, Arthur Orton (to Mary Ann Loder), and the Defendant (early letters to Lady Tichborne, &c.), in facsimile. In wrapper, price 6d.

BALAK AND BALAAM IN EUROPEAN COS-TUME. By the Rev. JAMES KEAN, M.A., Assistant to the Incumbent of Markinch, Fife. 6d., sewed.

ANOTHER ROW AT DAME EUROPA'S SCHOOL. Showing how John's Cook made an IRISH STEW, and what came of it. 6d., sewed.

Samuel Tinsley, 10, Southampton Street, Strand.

UNTRODDEN SPAIN, and her Black Country.
Being Sketches of the Life and Character of the Spaniard of the
Interior. By HUGH JAMES ROSE, M.A., of Oriel College, Oxford;
Chaplain to the English, French, and German Mining Companies of
Linares; and formerly Acting Chaplain to Her Majesty's Forces at
Dover Garrison. In 2 vols., 8vo., price 30s.

"The result of his observations is one of the most trustworthy and
interesting books upon Spanish life and manners in the southern provinces
during a period of great political disquiet that we have ever had the good
fortune to peruse. Evidently a gentleman and a scholar, with, in spite of
his profession, a dash of the sportsman, Mr. Rose combines the calm good
faith of the historian with the acumen of an advocate. . . . . We regret
that we cannot make further extracts, for 'Untrodden Spain' is by far
the best book upon Spanish peasant life that we have ever met with.
Valuable information is imparted in an honest, straightforward manner;
and nothing is exaggerated. Travellers proverbially tell strange stories,
but Mr. Rose has drawn upon fancy neither for his facts nor for his figures."
—Athenæum.

"The author of this work has proved satisfactorily that there was room
for another book on Spain. . . . It is fresh, life-like, and chatty, and is
written by a man who is accustomed to look below the surface of things."—
Standard.

"Leaving subjects worn threadbare, or touching them lightly, he
analyses in a way no one else has done the Spanish character. He has
looked beneath the surface, and he has seen for himself some of their
institutions. His sketch of domestic life in Spain is beyond praise. . . . .
We have rarely been able to recommend a book more cordially. It has
not a dull page, and no one can rise from its perusal without learning
more about Spain than he ever learnt by the most diligent perusal of
political letters from that ill-fated country. For our author (whose style is
good, method of arrangement lucid, and sympathies warm) not only is a
keen observer of things below the surface, but has the rare art of imparting
his information in a form alike pleasant and intelligible. The book
deserves to be a great success."—John Bull.

"An amount of really valuable information respecting the lower classes
of Spaniards, their daily life and conversation, and ways of looking at
things, such as few writers have given us. . . . . The second portion of
the book, which is devoted to the mining or 'Black Country' of Spain,
contains some capital sketches of character both of the Spanish miners and
of the Welsh and Cornish overseers and mining captains. . . . . In conclusion, we may remark that it is a work that should be read by everyone
interested in Spain, and in the moral and political crisis through which she
has been and still is passing."—The Field.

Samuel Tinsley, 10, Southampton Street, Strand.

www.ingramcontent.com/pod-product-compliance
Lightning Source LLC
Chambersburg PA
CBHW020901020726
47497CB00005B/1504